SARAH'S
CHRISTMAS
MIRACLE

MARY ELLIS

HARVEST HOUSE PUBLISHERS

EUGENE, OREGON

Scripture verses are taken from the *Holy Bible,* New Living Translation, copyright © 1996, 2004. Used by permission of Tyndale House Publishers, Inc., Wheaton, IL 60189 USA. All rights reserved.

Cover by Garborg Design Works, Savage, Minnesota

Cover photo © Chris Garborg

This is a work of fiction. Names, characters, places, and incidents are products of the author's imagination or are used fictitiously. Any resemblance to actual persons, living or dead, or to events or locales, is entirely coincidental.

The Baked Apples and Christmas Cake recipes come from *The Homestyle Amish Kitchen Cookbook,* Georgia Varozza, general editor.

SARAH'S CHRISTMAS MIRACLE
Copyright © 2010 by Mary Ellis
Published by Harvest House Publishers
Eugene, Oregon 97402
www.harvesthousepublishers.com

Library of Congress Cataloging-in-Publication Data
    Ellis, Mary
    Sarah's Christmas miracle / Mary Ellis,
        p. cm.
    ISBN 978-0-7369-2968-4 (pbk.)
    1. Amish—Fiction. 2. Christmas stories. I. Title.
    PS3626.E36S27 2010
    813'.6—dc22

                                                              2010012425

Printed in the United States of America

            10 11 12 13 14 15 16 17 18 / BP-SK / 10 9 8 7 6 5 4 3 2 1

ONE

The Day Before Thanksgiving

Why can't things remain the same?

As the sun rose over the eastern hills, the rolling, deep purple meadows glistened from a thousand sparkling prisms as sunlight refracted in the morning dew. Dawn was a magical time of day. Sarah Beachy shuffled her feet through shredded cornstalks as though she had all the time in the world. Fiery red and gold leaves swirled along the lane that separated their land from the neighbor's property. On her left stood the tidy white house and outbuildings of home—farmland that had been in her family for seven generations. The fenced pastures and rolling croplands stretched as far as the eye could see. On her right was her employer's business, Country Pleasures—a charming bed-and-breakfast on the county road. Two different worlds, but both dear to her heart.

Englischers came from all over Ohio to sleep on goose down pillows under handmade Amish quilts in antique four-poster beds. They ate hearty gourmet breakfasts in the luxurious dining room before setting out to visit Amish country. The community of Plain folk had drawn tourists for decades to the quilt shops, farmers' markets, and furniture galleries of Holmes, Wayne, and

Tuscarawas counties. Except for the danger from increased traffic, the Amish had adjusted to their newfound popularity while holding steadfast to their Christian faith and simple lifestyle.

Sarah enjoyed the best of both worlds. The farm where she lived with her parents and two sisters was within walking distance of the inn where she prepared breakfast, washed linens, and tidied rooms in between guests six days a week. *Englischers* weren't the only ones who were curious. Sarah loved hearing their strange accents, seeing their colorful combinations of clothes, and listening to breakfast chitchat about the bargains they had found at the flea market. And, because she usually finished work by eleven, the rest of her day stretched before her like a box of wrapped chocolate—each hour to be opened and savored at leisure.

"Sarah Beachy!" A voice broke through her trance. "Stop dawdling! I need you *today*!" Mrs. Pratt stood with both hands planted on her hips, yelling from the upstairs porch.

Although still too far away to judge facial expressions, she knew the innkeeper wasn't really angry. A kinder, gentler soul would be impossible to find. But she picked up her skirt regardless and ran the rest of the way—an unusual occurrence now that she had reached the dignified age of nineteen.

"You're not strolling woodland paths hand in hand with Adam. I need you to start an omelet while I fix fruit and oatmeal for the vegetarians and country fried steak for the men. I think the youngsters would enjoy Mickey Mouse-shaped pancakes." Mrs. Pratt's voice trailed off as she reentered the hallway, allowing the screen door to slam behind her.

Sarah smiled as she climbed the steps to the back door. *Strolling with Adam*…She thought she might do a little of that tomorrow after the big turkey dinner. The entire Troyer family had been invited to share the meal with the Beachys. Besides filling every chair around the ten-foot table in the kitchen, they would need to set up additional tables in the living room and enclosed porch. But as *mamm* planned to roast one turkey today and another tomorrow, there would be no shortage of food. Sarah hurried to wash up and put on her apron. When she turned from the sink, Mrs. Pratt held an upraised wooden spoon. "Are you going to smack me with that?" Sarah asked, trying not to grin.

"What?" Mrs. Pratt looked confused. "No, no. I'm trying to get a saucepan from the hook. Why Roy thought I needed this silly ceiling rack for pots and pans is a mystery to me. And I have no idea where my step stool is." At five-foot-nothing, Lee Ann Pratt needed her stool on a regular basis.

At five-foot-ten, Sarah almost never did. "Let me help." She stood on tiptoes and easily caught the handle of the sought-after pot.

"Thank you, dear girl. I'm so glad I hired someone tall." Mrs. Pratt bustled to the counter where cinnamon rolls were cooling on a wire rack. "Ready for the glaze," she announced, poking at one roll. "Please start an omelet for eight and get out some orange juice. We'll have to make do with frozen since there's no time to squeeze, but I've already sliced fresh pears and a pine-apple for fruit cups."

Back and forth the women buzzed around the room, like hummingbirds under the influence of fermented nectar. Sarah performed her duties with far less stress but no less efficiency. After all, keeping the inn filled to capacity with paying guests wasn't her personal worry.

"Everybody is in such a hurry today," Mrs. Pratt said, drop-ping her voice to a whisper. The first of the overnight guests had appeared and were headed toward the coffee service on the credenza in the dining room. "Folks want to pick up pumpkin pies and specialty gifts in town, or view the last of the autumn leaves before the holiday rush starts."

"Rush to where?" Sarah asked, dicing peppers and tomatoes for the omelet.

"Everywhere. People will be in a big hurry until Christmas, trying to finish their shopping, baking, and decorating. It never seems like there'll be enough time, but somehow there always is." Like a dervish, Mrs. Pratt grabbed her tray of fruit cups and marched into the dining room as though her bed-and-breakfast guests teetered on the edge of collapse from hunger.

Sarah smiled as the door swung shut. She loved working in the warm comfortable inn, especially because the frenetic innkeeper treated her like a daughter. From early spring through late fall, when the B and B operated at full capacity, her younger sister Rebekah worked there too. But as the holidays drew near and throughout winter, just Sarah and Mrs. Pratt ran the place like a well-oiled clock.

I hope the Englischers *won't be rushing around so much that they miss the point of the season*, Sarah thought. After putting bread in the eight-slice toaster, she added cheese to the omelet, turned the ham slices in the skillet, and stirred blueberries into the oatmeal.

"We need more coffee, dear," called Mrs. Pratt from the pass-through window. "And check the pancakes. Please don't let them burn."

"No problem." Sarah flipped the pancakes onto a platter and then peeked into the dining room before decorating the Mickey Mouse faces with licorice whips and pink frosting. Ten *Englischers*—ranging in age from six to seventy—milled around the table, talking, laughing, and sipping coffee from tiny china cups. Their clothes varied from blue jeans with missing knees to long print skirts, silky blouses, and high heels. Sarah loved being Amish, seldom coveting fancy clothes, but the odd combinations English women put together into outfits interested her.

How long does it take them to make up their minds each morning?

"They're ready for us to serve." The innkeeper breezed into the kitchen with an empty carafe in hand. Moments later the two women handled the culinary chaos of food allergies, restrictive diets, and peculiar taste buds with their usual precision. Soon, amid lavish praise and goodbye hugs, the guests departed to find their way down country roads, leaving Mrs. Pratt and Sarah with five rooms in disarray, a table full of dirty dishes, and a kitchen turned upside down.

But first they sat down to their own breakfast—something the proprietress had insisted upon since the day Sarah had been hired. They filled their plates from the serving platters on the table and then carried them to the nook overlooking the front garden. While they listened to birds bickering at the feeder or the clop-clop-clopping of horses and buggies on the road below, they shared a meal before readying the inn for the next onslaught of guests.

"Any reservations today?" Sarah asked, biting into a warm cinnamon bun.

"No, thank goodness. Because tomorrow is Thanksgiving, people will sleep in their own beds tonight or in the home of whoever is cooking the big bird." Mrs. Pratt took a bite of eggs and smiled. "It'll just be Roy and me for dinner. You'll be able to sleep in since I won't need you here, though I imagine your mother will have plenty for you to do."

"Hmm, *jah*, she will." Sarah sipped her coffee and watched

two cardinals squabbling at the suet feeder. "Why will it just be you and your husband? What about your children—aren't they coming to celebrate the holiday?" She set down her fork. Two people alone on Thanksgiving didn't seem right.

"No," Mrs. Pratt said, dragging out the short word. "My daughter lives in Baton Rouge with her three kids—too far to drive and too expensive to fly home. I'm hoping to see them at Christmas, but even that's doubtful. Her husband's afraid to take even a few days away with so many coworkers getting laid off at his plant. He plans to wait and see how things look the week before." She quickly ate another forkful of omelet. "Mmm, this does taste better with melted Swiss instead of cheddar. Good idea!"

Mrs. Pratt's brave effort hadn't fooled Sarah. Refilling both coffee cups, she said, "What about your son? Doesn't he live in Virginia? That's not as far away, is it?"

"He lives in northern Virginia, part of the suburban sprawl around Washington, DC. He has the opposite problem from my son-in-law. His company is so busy that people work seven days a week. Can you imagine going to the office even on the Sabbath? My son has so little time to himself that he'll never find the right person to marry unless some gal stalks him to and from Starbucks."

Both women shook their heads.

"He'll have Thanksgiving off, but he has to be back in the office on Friday. So he can't come home, either. I guess I should have had more than two kids. Maybe if I had four like your mom, I'd have a better chance for company during the holidays." She rose to her feet. "Eat more eggs," she ordered. "That's not enough to save, and Roy already ate cereal."

"No more for me, *danki*."

Mrs. Pratt ignored her refusal and promptly scraped the rest of the omelet onto Sarah's plate. "Nonsense, you're too thin. If we don't add some meat to your bones, you'll blow away when the wind howls across the fields this winter."

Sarah pushed the food around her plate with a troubled heart. Mrs. Pratt was acting cheerfully, but Sarah knew loneliness had arrived a day early. Without guests tonight, she and Mr. Pratt would have too much time on their hands. "Will you cook a whole turkey tomorrow for just two people?" she asked.

"A turkey? No, child. I bought the biggest chicken in the grocery store. I'll stuff her with sage dressing and roast her in the oven. Then we'll pretend she gobbled while walking the earth instead of clucking." She laughed while carrying her dishes to the sink.

Sarah ate another bite. Then she stood, took her own plate to the sink, and scraped the rest into the disposal. "Isn't there an English law that you *must* eat turkey tomorrow? Even if there isn't, I want you to join us for dinner. Believe me, we'll have more food than we'll know what to do with."

Her boss patted her arm before wiping down the stove and countertops. "That's very nice of you, but your mother doesn't need any more people in her house. If Adam brings the entire Troyer clan, you'll end up sitting on the steps and windowsills as it is." She reached for a large serving tray.

Sarah blocked Mrs. Pratt's path to the dining room. "Please, I want you to join us. It would mean a lot to me if you came."

For a moment the sweet-faced woman stared at her. Then she said, "All right, Sarah, thank you. But make sure you warn your family. My husband always makes a pig of himself with the candied yams. Better yet, I'll bring the yams myself so I will be certain there will be enough." She stepped around Sarah and began stacking cups and plates.

Sarah noticed two things different about Mrs. Pratt. Her left dimple had deepened, and she was singing along to the radio. Other than Sunday mornings in the church choir, the innkeeper hadn't sung since the Cleveland basketball team had made the play-offs.

Later, while Sarah stripped beds and ran the vacuum sweeper, thoughts of Mrs. Pratt ran through her head. *How can her children even consider not coming home for Christmas?* Other than attending church, how else would people celebrate the Lord's birth if not by spending time with family? Some folks' loved ones might have already passed on, or maybe they were never blessed with siblings or children, but how could a woman not see her grandchildren on Christmas morning?

Christmas Eve was the holiest time of the year. Everything seemed to look prettier, smell sweeter, and taste more delicious on that special night. Even the stars shone brighter in the night sky. Although Plain folk didn't decorate trees or their homes the way *Englischers* did, they enjoyed their own traditions. Since Sarah was a little girl, her *daed* would build up the fire in the woodstove after supper, and they would gather around to sing carols and eat Christmas cookies with tall glasses of milk. Later, he would read the story of Jesus' birth from his well-worn Bible. Gratitude for God's gift filled everyone's hearts when they finally crept upstairs to bed.

After she finished with her work, Sarah hugged Mrs. Pratt tightly, exacting a promise to come for dinner the next day. Joy from doing a good deed buoyed her spirits as she walked the back lane home. However, her pleasure lasted less than halfway. She remembered that only three of the four Beachy *kinner* would be at her mother's Thanksgiving table tomorrow. How quickly her brother had slipped from her mind, like a casual schoolmate who had moved to another county after graduation.

Caleb, quiet and sometimes sullen, spirited and temperamental, had left home five years ago and hadn't been back since. He'd been nineteen, Sarah's age, when he'd joined a construction crew headed for Cleveland. Caleb had grown rebellious during his *Rumschpringe*—arguing with *daed,* neglecting chores, and forgetting his Amish friends in favor of *Englischers* he'd met at work. Her father had assumed he would return when his work on the housing renewal project was finished. *Mamm* had assumed he'd come back once big-city excitement lost its appeal and he grew lonesome for his family.

Both had been wrong.

With tomorrow's big dinner and Christmas fast approaching, would Caleb's absence even be noticed in a house bulging with people? Or, like the prodigal son, would the absent child leave a void that those who had stayed behind could never fill?

Two

Thanksgiving Day

Whack! Adam Troyer split the log into two pieces with one precise swing of his ax. *Whack, whack!* Splitting firewood not only provided a toasty warm home but relieved aggravations that would otherwise turn him into a crabby man. He knew he had much to be thankful for, so why couldn't he utter even a single prayer of gratitude?

He had a good-paying job at a furniture plant specializing in solid oak tables, chairs, and bookcases. He had managed to keep his position during the recent round of layoffs. And he was courting the prettiest girl in the county. Tall and willowy, Sarah Beachy had flaxen blond hair and honey brown eyes that a man could get lost in. A half dozen fellows had sought to court her since the day she'd turned sixteen, yet she'd courted only him for the past three years. So why wasn't he happy?

Despite the fact that she was the usual age for Old Order Amish girls to become baptized and join the church, Sarah still hadn't done so. She hadn't even taken the classes in preparation. And whenever he broached the subject, she usually replied something like, "*Jah*, I've been meaning to do that..."

As though referring to mending a torn hem or oiling a squeaky door hinge.

Until she took her vows and joined the church, officially ending her "running around" years, they couldn't be married.

Adam had found the woman he wanted to spend his life with. At twenty-two he had already been baptized and joined the church. Because his job could easily support a family, Sarah wouldn't need to work at the English bed-and-breakfast. Mrs. Pratt might be a nice enough lady, but Sarah shouldn't be cleaning up after tourists when he was ready for a wife.

Whack! Like a well-oiled machine, he set log after log on the chopping block and split them into woodstove-sized firewood. He knew of no better way to burn off frustration over his current circumstances. With three older brothers, his father didn't need his help with farm chores, and because their family had been invited to the Beachys for dinner, there wasn't much to do inside the house, either. At least Thanksgiving was a paid day off.

Finally, by the time Adam had split half a cord of firewood, his anger began to wane, and he felt ashamed of his impatience. As he headed to the house to wait his turn for the shower, he focused on how much he loved her and silently pledged to let nothing get him down for the rest of the day.

"Hey, Uncle Adam," said Joshua. "What did one yawning two-by-four say to the other two-by-four?"

As people crowded around the Beachy table for Thanksgiving dinner, his nephew was ready with a joke. Adam smiled at his brother James' youngest son, a clever seven-year-old with flaming red hair. "I don't know," he answered, spooning cranberry

13

sauce onto his plate. Only half of the platters and bowls had made their way around the table, yet his plate was nearly full.

"I'm board stiff," the child sang out and then laughed uproariously, as did his siblings.

"Good one," said Adam, smiling with affection.

"I have another!" Joshua cried, waving a Brussels sprout on his fork like a banner. "What did the hammer say to the nail?" Without waiting to be prompted, he cried, "My, you've got a flat head!" As he delivered the punch line, the Brussels sprout flew off his fork and landed in the bowl of mashed potatoes.

Adam chose not to encourage the child further as both Adam's father and his brother instructed his young nephew on proper mealtime behavior. Instead, Adam stole a glance at Sarah, who sat across the table, seven people down. At least they were in the same room. The crowd of Beachys, Troyers, and English neighbors had overflowed from the kitchen into the front room and onto the enclosed porch. Sarah's father had set up a portable wood-burner to keep porch diners from freezing to death.

Sarah met Adam's gaze with a warm smile. She enjoyed his eleven nieces and nephews as much as he did. She would make a wonderful mother some day…and that day couldn't come soon enough in his opinion.

"I said…more turkey, son?" his *mamm* asked, finally getting his attention. She held out the platter with one hand.

"*Jah*, please." He reached across and speared two slices of thigh meat.

"There's only one thing that could take Adam's mind off this delicious meal," teased one of his sisters-in-law.

All gazes fastened on Sarah.

"Would that be the apple and pumpkin pies to come later?" Sarah asked, blushing to her earlobes. "He does love dessert."

"If Adam's not careful, he'll be the last Troyer to get hitched," said one of his younger sisters. "Now that we've announced our engagement, that only leaves Rosie, and she's just fifteen." Amanda smiled at her beau, who sat directly across the table.

Adam's siblings never overlooked an opportunity to needle Sarah about her hesitancy to set a wedding date. "All good things come to those who wait," he said, shooting his sister a frosty glare.

"Well, you've honed the virtue of patience to an art form," said Amanda.

"I'll tell you what's an art form...these biscuits," said Sarah, deftly changing the subject. "I love how the cheese melted throughout the dough." She broke a biscuit in half to reveal swirls of cheddar to her employer. "Have you tried one yet, Mrs. Pratt?"

Soon the basket of biscuits stood empty, and the conversation shifted to recipes on the women's side of the table and preparing fields for winter on the men's side.

Adam had eaten his fill of turkey, dressing, potatoes, and vegetables. Pie and coffee would have to wait. As the men wandered off to the porch and the women began clearing the table, Adam stopped Sarah in the doorway from the front room. "How about taking a drive with me? All the leaves aren't down yet, so there're still some pretty oaks by the old mill."

Sarah tried to step past him, but he blocked her path. "What kind of daughter would I be if I left this mess for my sisters and *mamm* to clean up?" She turned her dark eyes up to meet his.

"I thought with seven Troyer females to help, there wouldn't be room for everybody in the kitchen." He stuck his hands under his suspenders, suddenly self-conscious.

"I'll do my share and then come outside when I'm finished." She squeezed by, carrying a stack of dirty plates.

His three sisters and three sisters-in-law hadn't missed this verbal exchange. They rotated their heads back and forth like owls in the rafters. Only his mother didn't appear concerned with his love life.

"I'll be out in the barn whenever you're ready," he called as he headed for the door.

For the next hour, he listened to his *bruders* talk about the winter wheat crop, nearly dozed off while his father looked at threshing implements with Mr. Beachy, and then refereed a game of dodgeball among the *kinner*. Finally, Sarah appeared on the back porch. She stood tall and straight in her cornflower blue dress and white prayer *kapp*. Then she hurriedly put on her black wool coat and heavy outer bonnet, but for a fleeting moment Adam glimpsed what she might look like on their wedding day.

How I love her. I will develop the patience of Job if only one day she will be mine.

"I'm ready for that ride now that everything's straightened up inside," she said, walking toward him with cheeks pink from the chilly wind.

"Still plenty of daylight left." He helped her into the open carriage. The horse, which had been standing for an hour, stamped his hooves impatiently and snorted puffs of water vapor. As Adam released the brake, they took off down the driveway at a brisk trot.

Sarah scooted closer on the seat and tugged the lap robe up to her chin. "My, Amanda does love to talk, doesn't she? She dispensed advice on cooking, canning, and cleaning as though we Beachys had never used a rolling pin or pressure cooker in our lives." She winked slyly. "One would think she was a longtime matron instead of a bride-to-be."

"Ah, that would be my sister." He shook his head. "Whatever you do, don't start her on the subject of potty training."

Sarah hooted with laughter. "*Danki*, I'll keep that in mind. You should have heard her instructing my employer on laundry stain removal and how to get out melted candle wax. Mrs. Pratt has been in business for twenty years and has received three stars in English travel guides. Folks come from all over the state, Canada, and even from out West to stay at Country Pleasures. Newspapers in Cleveland, Akron, and Columbus write articles about her every year. She once showed me a scrapbook filled with glowing publicity."

"Is that right?" Adam turned off the county road onto a seldom-used gravel lane and then slowed the gelding's pace.

"And her recipes," Sarah enthused. "She's had them published in tons of cookbooks."

Adam rolled his eyes. "How many different ways can a person fix bacon and eggs or flapjacks?"

"You're joking, right?" she asked, turning toward him. "Mrs. Pratt knows at least a dozen different pancake batters. Besides, breakfast is more complex than that. We also make omelets, soufflés, quiches, and cheese stratas."

He stifled a yawn. After consuming so much food, cooking and recipes were the last things he wanted to talk about.

"And Mrs. Pratt doesn't just fix breakfast. She caters small wedding receptions, bridal showers, and family reunions. With prior arrangement, she'll even prepare elegant candlelit dinners with prime rib and twice-baked potatoes."

"Why would anyone bake a tater twice?" Adam asked, slowing the horse to a walk as the road turned to follow the river. Swamp willows along the bank still had their shiny yellow leaves, while the majestic red oaks displayed full autumn foliage.

"It's just a fancy way of fixing them." Sarah reached for a low-hanging branch as they passed beneath a tree. A shower of dead leaves rained down on their heads.

"You said the key word...fancy. Why go to all that trouble to make supper?"

"But doesn't dining by candlelight on a flagstone patio sound romantic? Then, during the winter, she puts tables-for-two in front of her living room fireplace and turns down the electric lights." Sarah released a wistful sigh and folded her hands atop the lap robe.

Adam bit the inside of his cheek. He refused to show an ounce of irritation, but he didn't like Sarah rambling on and on about the English inn. What did Plain folk care about soufflés and multibaked spuds? She'd once told him that she folded bath towels to look like swans when she made up a room. That was almost as stupid as streams of water hitting you from every side of the tub when a person took a bath.

"I'll tell you what's romantic," he said, choosing a patient tone of voice. "This place right here." He pulled on the reins. "Whoa," he called to the horse. The buggy stopped in front of an abandoned gristmill. The rusty waterwheel had locked for all eternity into one position. Someone had thrown plastic sheeting over holes in the roof and latched the shutters over broken windowpanes to slow the damage. Entwining ivy and wild grapevines softened the effect of years of deterioration. "It's hard to imagine that this used to be the center of our community." He plucked a tall purple weed up by the roots.

"This is a pretty spot," she agreed, glancing around. A smile turned up the corners of her mouth. "I love the sound of water rushing over the falls." She jumped down from the buggy without help and walked to the massive slabs forming the chute.

Adam tied the horse to a pine sapling. "Careful," he warned as he approached. "Those mossy stones can get slippery." He pulled her back from the edge and wrapped his arms around her.

She laid her head against his shoulder. "Did you know that Mr. and Mrs. Pratt would have been alone today if I hadn't invited them? Neither their son nor daughter could come for Thanksgiving. And they might not even make it home for Christmas, either." She clucked her tongue against the roof of her mouth.

"You have a kind heart, Sarah Beachy." Adam nuzzled his chin on the top of her head. To do so, he'd moved one step higher because Sarah was at least an inch taller than him.

"It sure would bother *me* if my children didn't come home on the holiest night of the year." Her voice wafted into the chasm and echoed off the walls.

He tightened his embrace. "Maybe the holiest night of the year isn't a big deal to the *Englischers*."

"But it is…Mrs. Pratt loves Christmas. She sings in her church choir and talks about their musical cantata all the time."

Adam clamped down on his back teeth. "If it's that important, I'm sure they'll work something out. And we'll raise our *kinner* right, so they'll never want to be away from home." He turned her gently in his arms and then kissed her soft lips.

She returned the kiss with a shy smile. "I hope so."

But unless he was imagining things, she had shivered and pulled back imperceptibly, as though an icy wind had blown in between them.

Something is wrong.

Yet for the life of him, he couldn't put a finger on what it was.

THREE

Elizabeth Beachy looked over the shoulder of her youngest daughter and smiled. "Don't get too carried away with those thumbprints in your cookies, Katie. You don't want the jam falling out the bottom when you pick up the cookie. And you, Rebekah, leave some of those chocolate kisses for baking. You eat as many as you decorate with."

Both girls giggled as they nodded their heads.

Elizabeth loved this time of year when family and friends came to call, bringing sweet treats or healthy appetites. Not surprisingly, very little turkey and dressing remained from the feast two days ago. With that many hungry people—many staying the whole day—a huge amount of food had been consumed. But with so many women, the cleanup afterward hadn't been any trouble.

The Troyers were a good family—every one of them hardworking, respectful of elders, and committed to the Christian faith. As far as she knew, none had caused much heartache to their parents, not even during *Rumschpringe*. Adam Troyer would make a good match for Sarah, although she had initially been surprised by her daughter's interest in the solemn furniture maker. Frivolous thoughts never crossed Adam's mind. He'd once mentioned that he scheduled his entire day after morning prayers, planning even a swim in the creek or a visit to a neighbor.

So very unlike my eldest daughter.

Sarah could be distracted by just about anything. Once she burned loaves of bread to cinders after hummingbirds in the morning glories had captured her attention. Another time she'd walked to town for toiletries but wandered into the library instead. After losing track of time, she ended up coming home without her drugstore necessities. Dreamy and sensitive, kind and gentle, Sarah returned wayward turtles to the pond, captured ladybugs on the screen to free outdoors, and rescued skunks that fell into the window well.

It had been Adam's kindness to a litter of abandoned cats that had first attracted Sarah. The two had spent hours feeding kittens from a baby bottle after a Sunday preaching service. Sarah had taken the brood home, but Adam came each day to help and then found them all good homes. Perhaps his serious nature might offset Sarah's absentminded one, although she appeared to be in no hurry to tie the knot.

Working at the bed-and-breakfast had done her a world of good. She'd grown more reliable, managed her time better, and had learned to handle money without elevating its importance. However, her *daed* would be quick to disagree. Eli thought she spent far too much time analyzing *Englischers* and held the inn responsible for her continued singleness.

Elizabeth had learned firsthand that you shouldn't force young people to do things against their will. You could instruct them and try to encourage, but in the end each must make up his or her own mind. To remain Amish was to place God first and yourself second, and that decision had to be personal. Someday Sarah would be ready to become a wife and mother.

Until that day came, there wasn't a thing her parents could do but pray.

"When will Sarah be home?" asked eleven-year-old Katie. "She loves to make cutout cookies, and we've already finished making the others."

"That's because she likes to eat the frosting," said fifteen-year-old Rebekah.

"I wouldn't talk if I were you," said Elizabeth, pulling back the kitchen curtain to peer outside. "Count the candy wrappers and then look at how few ended up in cookies."

Like clockwork, she spotted Sarah sauntering down the private lane that connected their township road to the county highway. Sarah carried her outer bonnet in hand, had left her wool coat unbuttoned, and appeared to be traversing the path instead of walking a straight line. Elizabeth set the kettle on the propane stove and lit a burner. By the time Sarah reached the house, apple cinnamon tea would be ready.

"I'm home," she called from the back hall. When she entered the kitchen, her face glowed from the cold. *"Guder nachmittag, schwestern."* Sarah greeted her sisters and tugged their *kapp* strings in succession. She buzzed a kiss across Elizabeth's cheek. "Have I missed the best part of cookie making?" She pushed up her sleeves and headed to the sink to wash. But instead of a using a towel, she shook the droplets of water over Rebekah's head. Rebekah responded by sticking out her tongue.

"Sit," Elizabeth ordered. "You're just in time." She placed the tree, bell, star, and heart cookie cutters in the center of the table. Katie grabbed the star, while Rebekah reached for the heart.

"Oh, good, I get to make green Christmas trees and silver bells this year—my favorites." This was always Sarah's reply, regardless of which cutters her sisters selected first.

Elizabeth rolled out the first batch of dough to the proper thickness, and then the three girls went to work. They had become experts in arranging the shapes for the maximum number of cookies. Any leftover scraps were rolled into balls, baked, coated with white icing, and dipped in sugar to make snowballs.

"*Mamm,*" asked Sarah, "what do you suppose Caleb is doing today?"

Katie concentrated on her placement of stars, but Rebekah looked up with alarm.

Elizabeth swallowed with a dry throat. "I have no idea. What made you think of your *bruder?*"

Sarah met her gaze. "I don't know. I guess I missed him at Thanksgiving dinner."

"With your boss here, plus a houseful of Troyers, you should have had plenty to keep you occupied." Elizabeth kneaded the next batch of dough with more energy than required.

"*Jah*, Adam's nieces and nephews are a handful, aren't they? I almost burst out laughing when that Brussels sprout hit the mashed potatoes. But I started to wonder what Caleb might be doing up in Cleveland. Surely he's not still working on that public housing project."

"If your *bruder* wanted us to know his whereabouts or how he's getting along, he would tell us." Elizabeth slapped the dough onto waxed paper, sending up a cloud of flour into the air.

Sarah cut out a perfect row of trees and then interspersed her bells between the hearts and stars. "Don't you have an address for Caleb? Some way to reach him in an emergency?"

Elizabeth stopped kneading and stared at her daughter as exasperation inched up her spine. However, Sarah sat transferring trees one by one to the baking sheet, unaware of the distress she had caused. "I have no address for him. He's not interested in our family emergencies, or he wouldn't have burned that bridge years ago." She began rolling out the ball of dough, pouring her irritation into the effort to avoid losing her temper. When she'd finished and lifted the rolling pin, three pairs of eyes were staring at her.

Sarah spoke in a gentle voice. "*Mamm*, that dough is too thin to cut out. Let me roll the next batch."

Elizabeth gazed down at the table and saw that she had rolled the dough paper-thin. Not sure if she should laugh or cry, she chose the former, to the great relief of two of her girls. Katie and Rebekah giggled good-naturedly.

But Sarah, looking concerned, reached over and clasped her hand. "Did I upset you? That wasn't my intention."

Elizabeth fought back the sting of tears and the egg-sized lump in her throat. "I suppose it's normal for you to be curious about Caleb." She had said his name, a hard thing to do as her husband refused to even mention the word. "I think about him from time to time, especially around Christmastime. But thinking doesn't change things, and dwelling on the one who flew the nest might make me lose sight of the fledglings who have stayed." She forced a smile and scraped the dough back into the bowl. "Let's put this into the refrigerator for a while to make it easier to reroll. Otherwise it'll be too sticky."

When she returned to the table, the younger girls had started frosting the first batch of cookies from the oven, but Sarah was still watching her. Elizabeth grabbed the bag of flour to measure out the next batch of dough.

"I thought you had an address and phone number where he could be reached," said Sarah. She acted like a stubborn dog, refusing to let go of his end of the stick.

Elizabeth released her best weight-of-the-world sigh—the

one mothers used to discourage additional comments or questions. But this time, the sigh failed her. Sarah merely waited with a spatula in one hand and a cookie cutter in the other. "We *had* his address and phone number, but when I wrote to him after six months, my letter and all thereafter came back marked 'Return to sender—no forwarding address.' And when I called, the number had been disconnected, and 'no further information is available.'" She heard the recorded message ringing in her ears as though it were yesterday. "That was the end of it. It was his choice. Now, if you don't mind, I'd like to change the subject. No sense talking about something we can't do anything about." She hadn't meant to raise her voice. Making cookies with the girls was one of her favorite holiday pastimes, but suddenly her harsh words echoed off the kitchen walls.

Sarah looked as though she might cry. "Sorry, *mamm*," she whispered.

Elizabeth felt worse, if that was even possible. "No harm done. I'm going to the cellar to see if we have any apricot preserves left. Why should all the thumbprints be strawberry?" She winked at Katie.

Once she was away from the overheated kitchen, she exhaled slowly. After all these years, the subject of her errant son, the one who had broken his parents' hearts, still hurt.

Will I never be able to let go of my anger and disappointment? Will I never be able to accept Caleb's rejection of the Amish way of life? Why can't I surrender my son to God and let the One who sacrificed His own Son care for him?

Memories of the year before Caleb left came flooding back, ripping open old wounds. By eighteen, Caleb was pushing every limit and breaking every rule set for him. He took to staying out late with his English friends, drinking beer and playing loud music at bonfire parties down by the creek. He'd gotten his drivers license and had bought an old pickup truck. When his father tried to clip his wings, he'd only grown more belligerent.

This is my Rumschpringe. You'll not tell me what to do!

His father had washed his hands of him. Then Caleb left for Cleveland on what should have been an eight-month construction project. Elizabeth had had a bad feeling when her son took an apartment close to Lake Erie with three other carpenters, all *Englischers*. He didn't come home on weekends as promised, and he didn't write or call to keep them from worrying.

By December she knew…he was never coming back.

Most young Amish men test the waters or try a little Englishness before joining the church and settling into the Plain lifestyle, but Elizabeth had known it would be different with Caleb. And that difference separated him forever from his family.

She hadn't forgotten her eldest son as she implied to Sarah. Memories of him would forever remain in her heart—a quiet, dull ache until the day she died.

FOUR

Mondays were usually slow days at work, and today was no exception. Country Pleasures seldom had guests on Mondays, especially not in December. Although city folk loved winter getaways, they usually arrived on Wednesdays or Thursdays and stayed for long weekends. Nevertheless, Sarah hitched up the buggy and drove to the inn. Mrs. Pratt kept several ponies in the fenced paddock close to the house to offer pony rides to children during milder weather. Because Sarah's mare got along with any equine breed, she turned the horse out to graze on sparse grass but plentiful hay.

"You drove to work today?" Mrs. Pratt asked when Sarah walked into the kitchen. "Afraid of a little exercise on such a beautiful day?" She handed Sarah a cup of coffee fixed how she liked it—with plenty of milk and two sugars.

"*Jah*. I have an errand to run after work, so bringing the buggy spares me a walk back home."

Mrs. Pratt's forehead furrowed with creases. "Where are you going, child? I'd be happy to drive you and get away from the house for a while. Besides, there's always something we need on the shopping list."

That is so like my boss...always eager to help a neighbor even with a list of chores planned for the afternoon. "No, *danki*. I'm not going far. Just to visit a friend." Sarah smiled and then finished her coffee in two long swallows. "Will there be guests tonight? Did you have any last night?" She peeked into the dark, empty dining room. She never knew what she would find on Mondays because she never worked on the Sabbath. Mrs. Pratt's sole helper that day was her husband—a dear man, but not blessed with a single domestic ability.

"Nobody's here but us mice, and I have no reservations for tonight." Mrs. Pratt opened the refrigerator door and bent over to look inside. "I know there's fresh fruit in here somewhere."

"Well, what shall we do today?" Sarah asked. They usually tackled major cleaning projects while the rooms stood empty.

"I think we should wash windows before it turns any colder. But first, let's eat! How about oatmeal?" Mrs. Pratt found the tub of blueberries she'd been hunting for and straightened her spine.

"Of course. I'll get it started," said Sarah. They always had oatmeal on slow days, topped with fruit or cinnamon and brown sugar.

During the meal they chatted about the weather, their plans for the upcoming weekend, and the local Christmas displays. Although Sarah loved the manger scenes and electric candles flickering in the windows, to her most of the plastic inflatables seemed silly. They were usually lying face down in front yards as though exhausted by their efforts.

After breakfast, while they washed dishes together, Mrs. Pratt again offered Sarah a ride. She felt guilty about her little white lie because she didn't plan to visit *her* friend but one of Caleb's. And it hadn't been her only deception that day, either. She had also led her mother to believe she would be visiting Josie instead of merely passing by on her way to the Sidley house. Albert Sidley had been Caleb's only Amish friend after he'd started working for the English construction company. If anyone knew her *bruder's* whereabouts, it would be Albert, but after five years it wasn't likely.

Yet how could she have told her mother the truth? Sarah had seen how upset *mamm* had become with questions about Caleb. She'd specifically asked Sarah to drop the subject. Why hadn't she realized her mother still suffered from him leaving the Order?

I've been too preoccupied with my own life to notice another person's pain.

She sent up a silent prayer of forgiveness for her deception and for her self-absorption. If she could obtain Caleb's current address and perhaps a phone number, maybe her mother wouldn't feel cut adrift from her firstborn. Knowing a person's whereabouts, or having the ability to call in an emergency, gave a person security... even if you never chose to write or call in the foreseeable future.

After the two women had washed the windows with vinegar water, Sarah ran the sweeper and dusted. A few hours later, with the inn clean and sparkling, she hitched up her horse and headed toward Caleb's former best friend.

Small by Amish standards, the Sidley farm stood on one of the last unpaved township roads. Sarah's buggy bounced from side to side for a mile and a half. Just when she thought her kidneys might suffer permanent damage, the one-hundred-fifty-year-old farmstead loomed into view, the last house before the dead end. She remembered visiting here once a long time ago, and her response remained the same—sheer pity.

Mrs. Sidley had passed away after the birth of her fourth son. Her husband and four boys scratched out a bare living on twenty hardscrabble acres of hilly, rocky ground. Even the three dairy cows looked forlorn as they chewed their cud beside the sagging fence.

Sarah drove up the rutted driveway, got out of the buggy, and tied the reins to the barn's hitching post. The house, in desperate need of paint, looked empty. Then Albert Sidley walked onto the rickety porch.

Why is it that some homes look full of life even when owners vacation, whereas this house seems empty while inhabited? It appears to suffer from a terminal illness. Sarah tried to put these thoughts away as she stepped forward and stood in the thin sunlight.

At first Albert didn't seem to recognize her. Then, "Sarah? Sarah Beachy?" he asked, walking down the steps. His wool chore coat was frayed at the hem and sleeves, while his boots were caked with dried mud. And he had come *out* of the house in those boots.

"*Jah*, it's me. I'm surprised you remembered." She forced a nervous smile.

Albert took a handkerchief from his back pocket to wipe his mouth and hands. "Of course I remember you. Hasn't been all that long." He approached with uncertainty. "Are you lookin' for my pa?"

"No, I was looking for you." She stepped closer and ran her sweating palms down her skirt. What had seemed like a good idea this morning no longer did. Her courage began to wane. "I'd like to talk to you about my *bruder*."

Albert squinted at her, though the sun had disappeared behind a heavy bank of clouds. The sunny morning had changed into a gloomy, overcast afternoon. "Caleb?" he asked. "What would I know about him? It's been four years or so." He shuffled his boots in the dirt. Driveway gravel had long ago sunk beneath a layer of mud.

"Five years, actually, but you were his closest friend, Albert. He trusted you and confided things he didn't tell his family."

"That was a long time ago, Sarah. After he took up with those carpenters, he didn't have much use for his old friends." The pain of rejection could still be heard in his words. "He let me try my hand at carpentry one summer on his crew. They were building barns for Amish and English. I wasn't any good with math, so the foreman wouldn't hire me permanently with all that measurin' and firgurin'. They wanted everything exact, and I had made a couple bad cuts. He said the next time I cut a board short, the price of that piece of lumber was coming out of my pay." His mouth thinned into a sneer. "I don't know why you can't just lay one board atop another and cut it about the same."

Sarah had no answer to that, but she didn't wish to alienate the sole person who might be able to help her. If anyone in Fredericksburg knew Caleb's address, it would be Albert. "Well, that job didn't turn out so good for Caleb either, as far as his family is concerned."

He gazed off to where two dogs chased a rabbit across a barren cornfield. When the rabbit escaped down a burrow, the dogs pawed the frozen ground, yipping with dismay.

The Sidley harvest was sparse this year, judging by the number of dried cornstalks, she thought.

Then Albert returned his focus back to her. "What do you hear from him? How's he making out in the big city?" His tone had softened somewhat.

"We haven't heard from him since he left."

"That happens, I s'pose. My pa says not everybody's cut out to be Amish. Some ain't got the spine to turn their backs on the temptations of ease and comfort."

Sarah watched the two dogs lose interest and then trot off toward the barn. If lack of comfort and convenience was what it took for assurance of heaven, the Sidley family had an easy path. But discussing salvation would be better left to the bishop or deacon. "Maybe so, but I'd still like to talk to him."

Albert stared at her while scraping his boot toe in the dirt. "Can't help ya."

"Did he ever contact you after he left?" The question hung in the brittle cold air. Sarah could almost see his mind whirring with possible answers or ways to evade the question, yet somehow she knew he wouldn't lie.

"*Jah*, I heard from him once or twice. He sent letters to our post office box in town." Albert crossed his arms over his tattered jacket. Sarah felt a barrier was being raised. "But I never wrote back. What would I have to talk about with an *Englischer*? 'Cause that's what he was. Making that kind of money, driving around in his pickup truck, living in a place where you could look out and see some big lake. He'd said in the letter he was joining the carpenters' union. You got any idea what kind of money they make?" Jealousy flashed in his dull gray eyes.

Sarah shook her head. "Nope. I don't have a clue about union wages." What she found more unsettling was that Albert knew these details. He'd known things about Caleb that his family hadn't for all these years.

"That much money just makes it easier to get into trouble." He lifted his chin. "You go on home now, Sarah. Your *bruder* is better off forgotten." Albert turned his back on her and marched toward the house.

Sarah's belly churned as her only chance slipped away. "Wait!" she demanded in an unfamiliar voice.

He stopped and glanced over his shoulder.

"Please, Albert. Give me another minute." He turned around but didn't come back. "Those letters," she continued. "Do you still have them?"

"Sarah Beachy, there's no sense in—"

"Do you still have them?"

"*Jah*, I've got them. Couldn't bring myself to throw them in the woodstove like I should have. I never had that many friends." He met her gaze and then focused on the frozen ground.

His hollow eyes had bored a hole through her heart. Tomorrow she would talk to her parents or the bishop about ways to help the Sidley family, but today she had her own agenda. "May I see them, please? I would like the return address if there is one."

"It's been four years."

"I know that, but it's all I have."

Albert stomped into the house and slammed the door. The aura of abandonment returned to the farmstead. He was gone so long she began to think he wasn't coming back. Then the door creaked open and he reappeared. Sarah ran up the porch steps without hesitation.

He held up a hand. "Wait, girl. Caleb said in his letters that he didn't want anybody knowing his whereabouts. I don't owe him any loyalty, but I do want to know why you're so interested all of a sudden."

Sarah stood paralyzed. Now it was her turn to consider possible reasons and excuses, yet she knew only the truth would get her what she wanted. She sucked in a breath. "I'm thinking about getting married. It'd never bothered me much that he took off and broke my *mamm's* heart until now. I want to know *why* he left before I start having my own *kinner*." She looked into his eyes, and he stared back for a long moment.

Then he slowly extracted two folded envelopes from his coat pocket. They were wrinkled and smudged, but Sarah spotted handwriting she recognized in the upper left-hand corner: Cal Beachy, followed by the information she had come for.

Adam's trip home from work took twice as long as usual. His boss let him go two hours early in exchange for making a delivery on his way home. Two hand-carved oak doors had been finished that afternoon and were needed for Christmas. As the buggy rolled down a township back road, he had time to ponder possible gifts for Sarah. He could buy a quilt she'd admired in the shop in town, but he knew several quilts would be made for her as soon as they announced their engagement. He thought about the basket of bath salts, lotions, and powders she'd liked in the fancy gift shop, but would her father think that gift too frivolous from a man with serious intentions? He'd probably buy a cardigan sweater, something to keep her warm this winter—his usual gift of choice.

As the sun dipped below the horizon, he clucked to the horse to pick up the pace. At this rate it would be fully dark by the time he got home. He hadn't brought along battery-powered lamps for the back window, and his buggy had only red reflectors. Light snow began to fall as he spotted another buggy approaching the stop sign ahead from a gravel side road. He slowed his horse, though he had the right of way. Something about the horse and buggy even in the dim light made the hair on his neck stand on end. After another moment he recognized the driver pulling hard on the reins. His initial suspicion was correct—Sarah Beachy was turning from the gravel lane onto the township road.

Sarah. What on earth is she doing out here? His mind clouded for a moment as he tried to remember who lived down there. Then he remembered Albert Sidley, a tall, thin fellow who seldom smiled or socialized within the Amish community.

Why would Sarah be visiting another single man in the district? Was this why she was dragging her feet and wouldn't allow him to announce their engagement?

FIVE

"Cal! Cal, you in there?"

The incessant pounding grew louder, until Cal opened one eye and then the other. He had been dreaming that he was pounding in a dowel while straddling a barn beam. The season was summer; the sun felt hot on the back of his neck, and down below boys scurried to-and-fro delivering materials and hauling off debris. His father worked only a few yards away, securing the other end of the beam.

But the pounding wasn't from his hammer, and he wasn't in Fredericksburg, Ohio. Cal Beachy bolted upright and glanced around. He'd dozed off on his plaid couch in front of the TV. The game show of contestants trying to answer questions for great sums of money had lulled him to sleep. He hadn't known a single answer since he'd started watching the program. His mouth felt parched, his back was stiff, and if the apartment grew any colder, he could unplug the refrigerator.

"I'm not goin' away, so you might as well answer the door," a voice hollered.

"Yeah, yeah, I'm coming." He rose and walked with more stiffness than normal for a twenty-four-year-old. When he opened the door, his friend Pete Taylor stood glaring at him.

Without waiting to be invited in, Pete stepped past him into

36

the apartment. "Man, it's freezing in here. Is your radiator on the fritz?" He headed toward the living room's heat source and began banging on the iron pipes.

"Easy there before you bust something," Cal warned. "I have it turned down." He raised the thermostat one notch.

Pete rubbed his hands together and took a perusing scan of the room. "Man, this place is a dump. Whatever you're paying in rent, it's too much."

Cal peered around too, trying to view it objectively. "It's not so bad. I got the couch and chair for free. People moving away set them on the tree lawn."

"No kidding." Pete's tone didn't reflect much astonishment.

"And the TV was only thirty bucks. The bed and mattress were left behind by the previous tenants, same with the potted plants and the kitchen table." Cal strolled around the room stuffing empty soda cans, fast-food wrappers, and pizza boxes into a trash bag. He felt ashamed of his untidiness. When he glanced back, his friend was staring at him.

"You are joking, I hope. Tell me you're not sleeping on a mattress somebody didn't think worthy enough to take with them."

Cal shrugged. "I bought a new mattress pad, sheets, and pillows. That blanket is brand new too." He pointed at the bright yellow heap in the middle of his unmade bed.

Pete nodded, but his expression didn't change from utter disdain. "I hate to be the one to tell ya, but your plants are dead and that table only has three legs."

"What's up with you? You been watching *The Martha Stewart Show*? I'm sure you didn't stop over to criticize my housekeeping." Cal slumped down onto his lumpy couch.

Pete flashed a half smile and pulled up one of the kitchen chairs. "Nope, I didn't. I came to tell you I picked up work today at the union hall. A project manager needed four carpenters for a hospital remodel—that big hospital on Twenty-fifth Street that takes people who don't have insurance. It'll be at least a year of work at prevailing wage and full benefits. You could have signed up too if you'd been down at the hall this morning."

"Is that right?" Cal asked. "I'm happy for you, Pete." *Only I don't feel happy. I feel jealous and a little angry. How come jobs didn't come in during the countless hours I sat there?*

He'd been an apprentice carpenter for almost four years. He would have made full journeyman by now if the housing bubble hadn't burst and the banks hadn't run out of money to lend. No matter how many times folks explained the mortgage crisis, he didn't understand how the situation had caused construction to grind to a halt. But for whatever the reason, his big dreams of union wages with a pension plan and three weeks of paid vacation had been squashed.

"Why did you stop coming down to the hall?" asked Pete. "You won't find a job sitting around here watching game shows."

Cal felt a knot of resentment tighten in his chest. "I wasn't getting any work there, either. And paying bus fare and buying my lunch downtown was costing money."

"Bus fare? What happened to your truck? You loved that Ranger."

"*Ach*, I left it parked overnight where I shouldn't have and they towed it away. When the police ran the plates, they found out I forgot to renew the registration, so they impounded it. By the time I figured out where they had stored it, the daily impound fee had risen to six hundred bucks. All told, I needed almost a grand to get my truck back. I didn't have that much, and the truck wasn't worth it." Cal set his feet up on the wobbly coffee table, pushing aside a stale bag of potato chips.

Pete looked sympathetic. "Cal, why didn't you call me right away? I could have explained what was happening."

Cal shot to his feet. "What do you think I am, stupid?"

"You know I don't think that, but you haven't lived here long enough to learn the ropes. I would think if I went to live with Amish people, somebody would explain how things worked down there. I'm sure I'd have plenty of questions. It's nothing to be ashamed of."

Pete talked slow and easy. That's what Cal had first noticed when they had met on a hotel construction project in Sugar Creek. Nothing got his dander up. He went along with the flow, no matter what the boss said to do. And Pete was smart. He could read blueprints and mechanical schematics. The foremen never had to keep an eye on him. Cal hadn't been surprised when Pete made journeyman after only a two-year apprenticeship.

"I wasn't ashamed," said Cal. "They had switched off my phone. Apparently, I'd sent my money orders to the wrong address. Payments were supposed to go somewhere in Kentucky instead of the phone company's downtown office. They finally found the money orders, but then they wanted to add a service charge for turning the phone back on. I didn't bother." He stared out a smudgy window on the street below. Trash collectors were making their rounds despite a long row of parked cars along the street. They tossed empty cans back onto the sidewalk without caring where they landed.

Pete walked to the window and gazed out, placing his hand on Cal's shoulder. "I have extra money this month in case you need a deposit."

Cal stood like a statue as the world passed by on the street below. The English world, of which he'd only marginally joined the fringe. "No, thanks. Save your cash, Pete. I didn't use the phone much anyway. Don't know anybody to call 'cept you."

"What about that chick you were seeing? What was her name... Carol? Karen?"

"Kristen." Cal answered without emotion. For a moment he remembered his first summer in Cleveland when they had met. *Kristen.* With her shiny blond hair and green eyes, she'd worn tank tops so low cut that the lace of her bra sometimes showed. And her tight blue jeans had left almost nothing to a man's imagination. Yet his imagination still managed to work overtime. They had so much fun together—going to dinner, taking a cruise boat along the Cuyahoga River, and kissing at the top of the Terminal Tower.

"What happened to Kristen?" Pete stood waiting for an answer.

Cal's mind wandered back. "What do you think? When they laid me off, I didn't have much spending cash, and she lost interest fast. Girls up here don't consider taking walks to the lake, riding the train downtown, or sitting on the roof to watch the sun set much of a date."

"Some do," Pete said. "You need to meet a better class of females, old buddy."

Cal rolled his eyes, a mannerism he'd perfected since turning English. "Yeah, I'll get right on that."

"Speaking of walks...let's do it. Let's take a walk by the lake."

"It ain't across the street anymore," he snapped.

"I know that. I'll drive us over. No offense, Cal, but your apartment gives me the creeps. It looks like somebody elderly died here and you moved in as soon as EMTs carried the person out. And you haven't changed a thing."

Cal glanced around at his scavenged furnishings and headed

for his coat. Maybe a walk would do him some good. It sure beat falling asleep on his uncomfortable sofa.

Pete parked his SUV in the deserted lot. Cal looked out the window. To the left was the swimming beach, empty except for about five hundred seagulls standing in neat rows. During the summer months, families and couples set up chairs or spread blankets on the sand to spend a day in the sun. On the right, expensive boats of all shapes and sizes filled the marina, waiting to be taken out on smooth blue water. But today every one of them had been pulled up and stored for winter. Both sights never failed to fill him with longing.

Cal had never been sailing, but from the balcony of his first apartment in Cleveland he could watch them bobbing in calm water or sleekly racing with the wind on Sunday morning regattas. How free, how powerful a man must feel at the helm of a ship.

"No boats out today," said Pete, scanning the horizon as though he had read Cal's mind. "Weather's almost nice enough, but a storm could blow up in no time on a shallow lake like Erie. Did you ever hear of the *Edmund Fitzgerald*?"

Cal shook his head as they walked down the path spanning the beach area. Birds took flight just beyond their footfalls, annoyed by the intrusion. Pete launched into a story about an ore freighter that had floundered and sank during an early winter storm on one of the other Great Lakes. As interesting as Pete's tale was, Cal found his mind wandering to his first year in the big city and his even bigger plans. He had been so full of himself.

"The higher a man thinks he gets means that much longer his fall back down." His *daed*'s warning rang hollowly in his ears. Cal should have buckled down and taken night classes as his foreman had suggested. He'd needed to learn the building codes that *Englischers* were so fond of. He should have saved money when the paychecks were substantial instead of buying drinks in loud clubs for people he didn't know.

He should have made a better attempt to fit in with the other employees. If he wanted to live in the English world, he should have emulated their ways. People didn't like those who were different.

"And they all lived happily ever after," Pete concluded.

"Huh?" Cal's head snapped up. "Really?"

"No," Pete said, frowning. "Everybody died. All hands were lost at sea. What's the matter with you? They even wrote a song about that story."

"Sorry. I can't keep my mind on anything. Don't take it personally, Pete. Good story—as much of it as I heard." Cal jammed his hands into his pockets and stared out at the cold, gray water.

Pete pulled up his jacket collar and turned his back to the north wind. "You gotta show up at the hall at least three times a week, Cal. Otherwise, they consider it the same as refusing work and cut off your unemployment checks."

Cal released a bitter laugh. "I sure can't afford to let that happen. You think I live in a dump now? Just imagine my next place if I lose my benefits."

"Then you had better pull yourself together, man. Take a shower and show up at the union center. I'll pick you up at seven tomorrow so you don't have to take the bus." He slapped Cal on the shoulder. "Now let's go get something to eat, my treat. It's freezing out here."

Cal looked once more at Lake Erie, stretching farther than the eye could see. Somewhere beyond the lake lay Canada. Behind him, some seventy miles to the south, lay Wayne County—a place he was never going back to. "I'll be cleaned up and shiny as a new penny by six thirty. And thanks, Pete. You're a good friend."

SIX

With the address tucked safely in her purse, Sarah tried to calm her racing heart. She couldn't believe Albert had parted with the envelope. He had not, however, allowed her to see her *bruder*'s letters. No matter. She had no desire to see Caleb's private correspondence, only to learn his whereabouts. Albert had possessed two different addresses. Two letters had been mailed more than a year apart. According to the postmarks, her envelope contained his most recent address. *I will write to him—*

Suddenly, the sound of horse hooves on pavement pulled her from her plans. Some fool in a buggy was trying to pass her! It was dangerous enough when a car passed on roads without buggy lanes, but an Amish buggy? Even though the road ahead was flat and straight, a horse couldn't accelerate the way a motor vehicle could to clear the lane quickly. She tugged hard on the reins to slow her mare.

"Sarah!" A male voice called.

This particular fool apparently knew her. She glanced to the left and recognized the ruddy complexion of Adam, her beau.

"Turn into the next driveway," he called, slapping the reins against his horse's back. His buggy lurched forward and he passed safely.

She followed him into the next farm drive, which fortunately had a turn-around. Once the horses had stopped side by side, she leaned forward to find him grinning at her. "Have you lost your mind?" she asked.

Adam laughed, set the brake, and jumped down. "Maybe so, but I couldn't believe my good fortune in seeing you." He approached with flushed cheeks, wearing the scarf she'd knitted for him last Christmas. "I thought I would have to wait for Sunday's preaching service." He lifted his boot to her buggy's bottom step.

"It's a good thing someone wasn't driving fast from the opposite direction when you were on the wrong side of the road." She crossed her arms over her coat. "That was very foolish."

"I am a fool for love." He leaned in for a kiss.

She turned her face so he met her cheek instead of lips. "You'll have lots to be thankful for tonight in your prayers."

"I will," he agreed. "Say, where were you coming from? The only people I know on that old gravel road are the Sidleys."

She turned toward him again. "*Jah*, they are who I went to see."

He arched an eyebrow. "You went to visit Albert Sidley?" A muscle in his neck jumped while his jaw tightened. "Do I have something to worry about? Has another man stolen your heart?"

If he'd meant the questions to sound lighthearted and teasing, he did not succeed. But Sarah took pity on him. "No, Adam. I haven't fallen for Albert, but I am concerned about his family. I intend to ask my *daed* to speak to the bishop. They might need the district's help and are too proud to ask. That farm needs maintenance on the outside, and I would expect on the inside too. Plus, their cellar probably isn't well stocked since Mrs. Sidley's passing. To my knowledge, none of her sons has married." She smiled sweetly. "I think they could use a work frolic, and the district could stock them up with canned goods before winter."

Adam rubbed his stubbly chin. "That's a good idea." He waited to see if more was forthcoming. After a few quiet moments he asked, "But why did you go there in the first place?"

Sarah let out a great sigh. "If you must know, I went to see if Albert had an address for Caleb. He was my brother's only Amish friend after he started working."

Adam grit his teeth for no apparent reason. "And did he?" he asked.

"*Jah.*" She patted her purse. "I have his address in case *mamm* decides to write. She was feeling mighty blue the day we were baking Christmas cookies. Time doesn't seem to have eased her sorrow."

Adam leaned into the buggy and kissed her forehead. "You have a generous heart, Sarah Beachy. I'm a lucky man."

"That you are, but I want to get home before full dark."

He stepped back. "Good idea. I'll see you on Sunday. After the preaching service, we'll have the whole afternoon to visit." He smiled and then hopped up into his buggy. "I'll follow you until the turnoff."

"You just keep to your side of the road," she called before clucking her tongue to her horse.

They set off with Adam close behind her. Despite darkness and a light snow beginning to fall, Sarah felt safe and protected all the way home.

Second Sunday of Advent

The snow that had begun Saturday afternoon continued throughout the night. Sarah and everyone else in the county awoke to eight inches of fresh new powder. Fortunately, the hosting family, the Troyers, lived on a state route. The Highway Department snowplows had been out early clearing the pavement, so the Beachys, and most other district families, arrived at the preaching service on time.

As soon as *daed* parked their buggy, Sarah and her sisters jumped down and headed for the house. They each carried a basket with something for the lunch table. Rebekah had baked corn muffins, Katie carried *mamm's* broccoli casserole, and Sarah brought jars of spiced apple rings. Because the Troyer home was the largest in the district, they held church services in their front room instead of in an outbuilding. Adam and his brothers had already moved out the normal furniture and set up long rows of benches. As Sarah helped organize the food in the kitchen, she spied Adam passing out hymnals. He looked so handsome in his black vest, coat, and starched white shirt.

He winked impishly when their gazes met, and she quickly averted her eyes. With church about to start, she didn't need to be thinking romantic thoughts. *Not that anyone could accuse me of having overly passionate ideas.*

She thought Adam to be handsome, dignified, and responsible. By all estimates he would make a good spouse. So why hadn't she accepted his proposal and allowed their engagement to be announced? The problem lay with her. She wasn't ready to quit her job and start having *bopplin*…babies that could one day grow up to break her heart. Amish families set no store by fancy clothes, furniture, or personal possessions, but they did take pride in their children.

What happens if your son grows up and turns his back on the Amish way of life? Or the daughter you molded to be just like you runs off with an Englischer *and never looks back?*

A sour taste rose up Sarah's throat as she finished slicing pies and setting out desserts. When the bishop called them to worship, she tried to put aside her anxieties. Fear was the handiwork of the devil, but how did a person live a life without fear?

For the next three hours, she concentrated on the hymns, Scripture readings, and the two sermons. She loved Advent season—the weeks leading up to the celebration of the Savior's birth. The bishop's sermon focused on John, the son of Elizabeth and Zechariah, who had prepared the way for Christ. Never once had John allowed people to focus their attention on him. With Christmas less than three weeks away, hearing a story about selflessness helped prepare a Christian's heart. When Sarah thought about self-sacrifice, she thought of her mother. Everything Elizabeth did was for God or for her family.

When church concluded and folks lined up for the buffet, Sarah noticed that her mother was one of the last to eat. With a grumbling stomach, Sarah had been one of the first in line. Feeling slightly ashamed of her behavior, she took her plate of food to sit with Adam and his older brother and sister-in-law.

"How did the Beachys fare during last night's storm?" asked Adam, making room for her on the bench.

"All right," she said. "We all bundled up and helped shovel paths to the henhouse and the barn. The cows need to be milked no matter what the weather. Then we moved firewood onto the porch for easy access."

"Good thinking. Hey, did you make these spiced apples?" Adam popped a ring into his mouth.

"*Jah*, but that was last summer." Sarah bit into a piece of cold fried chicken.

Adam's sister-in-law grinned. "If you would have brought a bottle of catsup, he would have declared it the best catsup he'd ever tasted. A man in *liebe* tends to act like that." She smiled at her husband.

Adam squirmed while Sarah blushed, but fortunately they were interrupted. "Hurry, Uncle Adam. You don't want to miss the fun." Joshua Troyer pulled on Adam's elbow. Bundled in his coat, hat, and mittens, the child looked ready to play.

"Good gosh, Joshua. What about lunch? Have you eaten?"

"I ate already, and now we're going to build a snow fort. Come outside with us." The boy ran off to join his siblings and cousins as they pulled on boots by the door. Soon the group trooped out. Even the girls were ready for some fresh air.

"Apparently, not everyone looks on snow with a pessimistic eye like I do," Sarah said, sipping tea.

"They love it. If I'm not needed here, I think I will wander outdoors when I finish eating…just to supervise the *kinner's* play, you understand. Sometimes snowball fights can get out of hand without an adult nearby." Adam wiggled his brows.

Sarah watched him consume his plate of food in record time. He brushed a kiss across her cheek when no one was looking and then followed the last of his nieces and nephews. She savored a second cup of tea while doing the dishes. But when the other ladies headed to the front room to sew and chat, she chose not to join them. *Too many questions I would rather not answer.* Slipping on her heavy wool cloak, bonnet, and gloves, she wandered outdoors. The sky had cleared after the storm. The sun sparkled off a world of white.

The young male Troyers had erected two snow forts about twenty-five feet apart. They would periodically stand up to lob snowballs into the other fort. Adam and his brother were busy building the forts higher and sturdier, each taking their share of direct hits. A coating of snow covered their hats and jackets.

Sarah hurried around the house before anyone spotted her and began hurling snowballs in her direction. In the front yard she found activity more to her liking. The little girls were building a snowman. They had already rolled the giant bottom ball and also the middle sphere. Only the best part, the head, remained. The girls invited Sarah over to help, so she went in search of stones for his buttons near the foundation of the house. By the time she returned, they were setting the snowman's head in place. One niece had procured a carrot for his nose, another found an old straw hat to keep his head warm, and a third cleverly added straw for his beard. One older niece lifted up the youngest one so she could line up coals for his mouth and nose. And not one of the children bombarded another with a snowball as they worked!

"I see the girls are behaving better than the boys," came a voice over her shoulder. Adam had crept up during the snowman's final adornments.

"Perhaps *this* supervisor encourages a more peaceful play atmosphere," said Sarah.

"That might have something to do with." Adam encircled her waist with both arms and hugged tightly, despite their heavy layer of clothes.

"Do you think he needs a coat, Aunt Sarah?" asked the tallest niece.

"No, dear. He'll be fine with just the hat."

"*Aunt* Sarah?" Adam whispered in her ear. "How do you like the sound of that?"

"It sounds as though she's putting the cart before the horse." A well-placed elbow connected with his ribs. "Let's get these kids inside to warm up before they catch colds." She swung the youngest girl up to her hip and herded the rest toward the house.

Adam nodded, lifting up the second smallest child.

In truth, Sarah didn't know how she felt about it. Becoming their aunt meant becoming Adam's wife. And as fond as she was of him, she wasn't ready for her own home and children yet.

Too many heartaches lie in wait down that road.

SEVEN

With his chores finished, Adam dressed warmly that morning, combing his hair and shaving with the utmost care. He would see Sarah that afternoon for the third time within a week. An ice skating party had been planned for today as soon as the forecasters predicted that the cold snap would continue.

A Wednesday get-together wasn't a problem for most Amish young people, who either farmed or were somehow connected with agriculture. Although barn chores continued year-round, farm fields buried beneath a layer of snow eliminated the most time-consuming tasks for farmers. Not so for Adam. A furniture maker's job didn't depend on seasonal cycles of planting and harvesting. However, he had two weeks of paid vacation, and his boss allowed him to take days off on short notice so he didn't miss every social event.

Upon his suggestion, Sarah agreed to come skating, even though she wasn't fond of winter activities. Mrs. Pratt would drop her off at the pond behind the schoolhouse on her way to a dentist appointment, and Adam planned to drive her home afterward.

Tonight he wanted to bring things to a clear understanding between them. He loved her. He saw her warm smile each night when he closed his eyes, and her sweet face greeted him every morning. They were meant for each other. Their families approved of the match, and he possessed the wherewithal to support a family. They weren't too young. She had no elder sisters who should wed first. And they got along well, never bickering the way some couples did. Sarah might be unsure of herself, but he possessed enough assurance for both of them.

His only concern was his delivery. Adam knew that women liked a little romance while courting and, unfortunately, although his skills as a master craftsman landed him the best contracts for custom cabinetry in restaurants and galleries, he was far less proficient with speaking his heart.

When he arrived at the pond, the skating party was in full swing. Most of the scholars hadn't gone home after school but had stayed for the festivities. Boys were separating into two teams for a hockey game, with straw hats versus black hats distinguishing the sides. Some of the hockey sticks had been store bought, but Adam had crafted his stick from hickory. After tying up his horse and setting out a bale of hay, he grabbed his skates and headed toward the sound of laughter. Because he didn't see Sarah among the girls already skating or huddling close to the bonfire, he had time for some male camaraderie.

"Adam, over here," hollered a friend. "We're a man short on our team."

He laced up his skates, turned up his collar, and glided over to join the game. The ice had frozen thick and glassy over the pond's deep end, offering a smooth surface for skate blades. Early arrivals had swept the surface clear of snow with giant push brooms. Unlike Sarah, he loved winter. With the wind whistling in his ears, skates scraping on ice, and shouts of encouragement from his teammates, Adam never grew cold because the fast action kept his blood pumping through his veins. Finally, the team captains called for a snack break.

Snacks? In his hurry to leave, he'd forgotten to grab a bag of chips or a tin of cookies. His thermos of hot coffee had doubtlessly grown cold by now. "I didn't bring anything to eat," he said as the men skated toward the bank.

"Don't worry," said one of his friends. "The gals always bring plenty. Rebekah Beachy brought a pot of sloppy joes, and Jessie Yoder brought corn dogs. Jessie kept the corn dogs warm with a battery-powered heating pad, while Rebekah kept her pot warm with hot coals."

Adam nodded, duly impressed with female ingenuity. But with the mention of her sister's name, Adam remembered Sarah and felt guilty. He'd played hockey for more than an hour and hadn't thought once of his girl. As the men approached the bonfire, where lawn chairs ringed the warmth, he spotted Sarah. With her hands beneath her wool cloak, her bonnet pulled forward to shield her face, and her skirt down to the frozen ground, Sarah Beachy was barely recognizable. She stood so still she could have been a female scarecrow, positioned to thwart scavenging crows.

"Sarah," he called while still several paces away.

She half turned, revealing a porcelain face with an expression of misery. "Hello, Adam. Lovely weather we're having, no?"

"Jah," he agreed, "but it would be nice to see the sun every now and then." He held out his palms to the roaring blaze. The heat began to seep through his soggy leather gloves.

She cocked her head to the side. "I was being sarcastic. It's colder than the North Pole out here and that wind nearly cuts a person in half." Several of her friends nodded in agreement and moved closer, as though closing ranks.

He regretted playing hockey for so long. Because he'd invited Sarah to the party, he should have been more aware of her comfort. "Let's get you warmed up near the fire," he said, taking her hand.

"I was standing closer, but the wind kept shifting and blowing smoke in my face. I feared the sparks would catch my cloak on fire. But then again, I'd no longer be cold, would I."

"Don't be such a complainer, Sarah," said Rebekah. "Adam didn't come over to listen to you whine."

Sarah's frozen expression altered as her jaw dropped open. "What do you mean?"

"It's winter, isn't it? Of course it's going to be cold today." Rebekah smiled sweetly while Sarah frowned at her sister. "Adam, have you tried my sloppy joes? The meat is still warm. I'll fix you and Sarah each a sandwich." She scurried off without waiting for a reply.

"Come with me, dear girl," said Adam. "Let's go to the other side of the bonfire, away from the sparks and from the others." He tugged off her mittens and started rubbing her fingers one at a time. "Hold your hands out to the heat. Is that better?" he asked after a minute, shielding her body from the wind with his.

"Much better," she said. "Sorry. Rebekah is right. I am a whiner. Better not ask me out again until April. I'm bound to be in a better mood by then."

"It's freezing out here if you're just standing around. Didn't you bring your skates? Will you try out the pond today?" He caught the scent of strawberries despite the tang of wood smoke in the air. Sarah used strawberry shampoo and body lotion.

She moved away from the blaze while slipping on her mittens. "*Jah*, I skated for a while with my sisters. Then my blade snagged a rough spot, and I lost my balance. I fell down hard on my backside without a shred of gracefulness. Rebekah said if

I kept that up, the ice would crack and everybody will fall into the water."

"Your sister is in rare form today. But you don't have to worry about the ice. The schoolteacher's father drilled a hole to gauge the thickness. He would have canceled the party if there was any danger whatsoever. This ice will support tons of weight."

"Well, thanks a lot, Adam Troyer. I feel much better now." Sarah huffed out a cloud of condensed vapor.

"You know what I mean. You're as skinny as a rake handle."

"A rake handle? My, you're just a real sweet-talker today, aren't you? You're doing my icy heart a world of good."

Adam swept off his hat and thumped it against his leg. "I'm sorry, Sarah. Let me walk to my buggy, come back, and start this afternoon over."

A slow smile pulled up the corners of her mouth. "If you head to your buggy, I'll be right behind you. Then we can go someplace warm." She turned her other side to the fire as though frying an egg.

"We can leave whenever you're ready," he said, tugging his hat back on. "I don't want you being miserable when this was supposed to be a fun occasion for us."

Her smile bloomed across her face. "*Danki*, but we'll stay a while longer. I can once again feel my fingers and toes. Let's eat those sloppy joes my sister fixed before they freeze solid. I've worked up a fierce appetite with my moaning and complaining."

Adam slipped an arm around her shoulder as they walked back to the group. *So like my Sarah.* Her sense of humor never failed to rescue him from some blunder or bad choice of words. And she wasn't afraid to laugh at herself. There wasn't a prideful bone in her body. Although she didn't need flattery or praise, he wished just once he could express how he felt about her.

Working in an all-male factory provided little opportunity to learn how other men conversed with women. He might be an expert with hand lathes, sanders, and every stain and wood preservative made, but with social conversation he was a dismal failure. Sarah occasionally eavesdropped on the guests' breakfast conversations at Country Pleasures. The bed-and-breakfast attracted business folk, doctors, nurses, and teachers on school break. She'd once served two college professors, a writer, and the governor of Ohio at the same meal. Those people knew how to string words together into a sentence.

Don't worry...this ice will support tons of weight.

An Amish woman might not be looking for glibness in a mate, but if he could express his heart, he might have an official fiancée instead of a beau.

"There you two are!" Rebekah called. "I fixed your plates. Adam, I gave you two sloppy joes because your hockey game must have worked up an appetite. How about a cup of hot chocolate?" She handed each of them a plate.

"Jah, danki," he said. The girl had heaped potato chips next to his sandwiches, but she had given Sarah only a few. As Rebekah hurried off to the folding tables, he and Sarah settled into lawn chairs by the fire. Adam transferred some of his chips to her plate.

She smiled, popping a chip into her mouth. "My sister must still be worried about the ice."

"I should have brought a bag of something," said Adam. "I was in too big a hurry to get here."

"Don't be silly," said Rebekah, appearing with two cups of cocoa. "There's plenty of food. Sarah brought Jell-O cubes, but I'm not sure who would want to eat Jell-O on a frigid day." Her words trailed off as she headed back to the group of girls.

"Now Rebekah seems to be worried about you," said Sarah. "She fears you'll waste away to skin and bones if we marry." Sarah blew lightly on the foam of her cocoa.

The hot chocolate chilled inside his belly, but he couldn't bring himself to say *If we marry, not when we marry?* "Let Rebekah worry all she wants. I'm not the least bit concerned." He reached for her hand, but she was holding both her plate and cup. "I've tasted your fried chicken and mashed potatoes—even my *mamm* makes none better."

"My sister says my mashed potatoes have lumps."

"Your sister has lumps in her head," he whispered by her ear, not certain if she'd heard him.

Her sly grin indicated otherwise. "That's what I've suspected for some time, but Rebekah is a better baker than me. You should taste her cheesecake and buttermilk biscuits."

Adam scowled, not wishing to discuss her sister or baking any longer. "Man does not live by food alone. She probably has no gift with *kinner*, while I watched you with my nieces last Sunday. You were so patient with them, encouraging their ideas instead of doing things for them." He sipped his drink, ending up with foam on his nose.

Sarah dabbed his face with her napkin. "Your nieces are little darlings. Being patient with them is hardly a challenge." She took a bite of sandwich.

"Even so, you're a natural with children. After you left, my eldest niece told me how much she liked you." He took a deep breath before continuing. "I wish your classes would start soon because I can't wait to make you my wife. You're going to make a wonderful mother someday, Sarah. And that day couldn't come soon enough for me."

The roaring bonfire, the skaters on the pond, and the woods

behind them turned eerily silent after he uttered the words that occupied his every waking thought. Or so it seemed to Adam. He'd finally found the courage to speak the words in his heart, and now it seemed that his entire life hung by a thread in the crisp December air.

Sarah wasn't quite so affected by his revelation. "Do you think so? Only time will tell about that." She rose to her feet and brushed crumbs from her skirt. "You know what? Too bad for the ice on the pond. I'm having another sloppy joe. That sandwich was delicious. And I'll bring you some Jell-O cubes." Off she marched to the snack table without a backward glance.

He might as well have declared his prediction for January snowfall, considering her reaction. *Am I beating my head against a door that will never open?* He could abide with her reluctance to commit. Becoming an Amish wife meant a lot of work and responsibility, but maybe her hesitancy was with him. Adam tossed his paper plate with the rest of the sandwich into the fire. His appetite had vanished.

Sarah had a kind heart. Maybe her sensitivity to his feelings kept her from admitting the truth…that she would never marry him.

EIGHT

Thursday Morning

Sarah arrived at work right on time. The inn would be filled with guests staying through the weekend. *Englischers* came down from Cleveland or up from Columbus to buy handmade quilts, crafts, pottery, and gift baskets for Christmas. Three couples had also arranged for candlelit dinners besides their complimentary breakfast. Mrs. Pratt would keep her busy preparing for tonight's dinner in addition to their regular duties.

But that was fine with Sarah. Unlike yesterday's skating party on the schoolhouse pond, the inn would be warm. Mrs. Pratt would light the fireplace, while bayberry candles and potpourri warmers would add holiday fragrance to the rooms. Sarah had slept under an extra quilt last night. The cold had soaked into her bones and wouldn't leave, despite Adam's tender ministrations. The bonfire had helped somewhat, but she would never be a fan of winter sports. She preferred curling up inside with a cup of ginger tea and a good book any day.

Sarah hung her cloak and outer bonnet on the hook by the door and walked into the kitchen. "Oh, good," said Mrs. Pratt as she flitted around the room in a tizzy. "You're here early. Hurry to wash up and get your apron on, dear girl. We have a barrel of monkeys today."

Sarah complied with a smile. A barrel of monkeys was Mrs. Pratt's favorite expression for multiple dietary requests from the guests. Without batting an eyelash, an innkeeper must learn to handle vegans, diabetics, and those who were lactose intolerant or required gluten-free fare. The two women served breakfast with their customary proficiency and then sent the guests on their way for a day of holiday shopping.

Sarah carried two mugs of coffee to their usual breakfast spot before going back for French toast. When she returned, Mrs. Pratt had settled in the chair next to the window. The slanted winter light revealed dark circles and deep creases around her eyes.

"You look tired," Sarah said. "Didn't you sleep well? Did Roy keep you awake with his snoring?"

"Nope, can't blame my husband this time." Mrs. Pratt sipped coffee and glanced down at her plate of food. The network of bright red spidery veins across her eyelids alarmed Sarah.

"Have you been crying? What's wrong? Is there something you'd like to talk about?" Sarah set down her fork.

"Just eat, child. I'm all right." Mrs. Pratt stared out the window at the low, threatening sky. "I talked to my daughter last night. She still can't tell me whether they are coming for Christmas or not. Her husband's still afraid to ask for time off. I'd like to know whether I should wrap the gifts for under the tree or pack them for shipping to Louisiana." She returned her attention to the table and buttered an English muffin fiercely. "If I press her to decide yay or nay, she'll just say they are not coming. Then I'll have cut off my nose to spite my face."

Sarah didn't quite understand the English expression, but

she caught the drift. "Perhaps you could wrap up the gifts fancy for under the tree, and then, if need be, we could pack them up for shipping at the last minute. If the gifts arrive after the holiday, so be it. You won't be there to see your grandchildren's faces during the unwrapping anyway."

Mrs. Pratt met her gaze over her coffee cup. "That's true enough, isn't it? I'll hope for the best, and if the worst happens, I won't worry if the presents are late." She ate her French toast with a bit more enthusiasm.

"It'll be a big deal for you if they don't visit, won't it?" Sarah asked the question, but she already knew the answer by the woman's expression.

"I can't believe I might not see my daughter and her family on Christmas! Some things should be more important than jobs and paychecks. Maybe they have bills to pay and obligations, but if you can't be close to your loved ones during the holidays, what's it all for?" She dropped her fork on her unfinished breakfast and rose from the chair.

Sarah glimpsed tears in her boss' eyes. "What about your son? Are you sure he's not coming either?" Her taste for food had also evaporated.

"Who knows? I called him on the phone and went straight to voice mail. I've sent him three e-mails and haven't received one reply. At least his present is always a gift card—no problem packing *that* up to send."

"I take it there are no reservations for Christmas Eve?"

"Goodness, no. I wouldn't take a reservation for that night even if I knew for sure my family wasn't coming. People should be with friends or family on Christmas. If Roy and I are alone, we'll go to church and then I'll sit by the fire reading my Bible until bedtime. For supper, I'll heat up something from the fridge.

It won't be the end of the world. You know I always have leftovers." She walked into the dining room with Sarah on her heels.

As they scraped and stacked plates into the tub, Mrs. Pratt began humming—a sure sign she was upset. Sarah racked her brain for something to lessen her pain but came up empty. Her own mood, so filled with joy that morning, soured to match Mrs. Pratt's. "Do you ever regret having kids?" she asked quietly.

"What kind of question is that? My goodness, Sarah Beachy, you do come up with some doozies." She carried the tote of dirty dishes back to the kitchen, while Sarah brought the tray of silverware and soiled linens.

Sarah watched her closely while they loaded the dishwasher. "So you never regretted becoming a mother?"

Mrs. Pratt's mouth opened with a ready retort, but when she saw Sarah's earnest face, she swallowed her words unspoken. After a moment she said, "No, I've never regretted having kids, not even when they disappoint or anger or frustrate me. I love them with my whole heart, unconditionally. Being a mother is no guarantee you won't ever be lonely, but our lives would be empty without the children and grandchildren. Even when they are far away and months go by without seeing them, they are always in my heart."

"That's good to hear." With a deep sigh, Sarah filled the detergent dispenser and closed the door.

"What brought this on? Are you getting nervous about marrying Adam? That's normal, but once the babies come along, I've never met a woman yet who wanted to send them back. Now, let's get started on the rooms. We have a can of worms today with three couples expecting a gourmet dinner." She purposely mispronounced the word "gurr-met," her pet joke.

But Sarah hadn't been reassured. While dusting, sweeping,

and cleaning bathrooms, she stewed about the dilemma every mother faced. She'd seen the disappointment on Mrs. Pratt's face over the prospect of an empty house on Christmas morning. And she knew her *mamm* faced painful memories. Although the Beachy home would be far from empty, Caleb's absence would be keenly felt.

When the rooms were tidied, Sarah helped in the kitchen making salads, baking bread, and peeling potatoes. She listened halfheartedly to Mrs. Pratt's chatter about the price of fresh vegetables during the off-season. When a lull in the conversation occurred, she rallied her courage. "I've been meaning to ask you something. If…if you had a friend's address in another town and wanted to find out exactly where he lived, how would you go about it?"

"I would drive to the town and then ask somebody where the street was when I got there. They might even know the person and direct me right to their front door."

"What about if you were looking for someone in a city like Cleveland?" Sarah placed the colander of potatoes under the faucet stream.

"Cleveland? Who in the world do you know up there?"

"My brother, Caleb. He moved there several years ago, and I'd like to know where he lives."

"Oh, that's right. I almost forgot. What made you think of him?"

"Folks are starting to forget him, and that shouldn't happen. He's my *bruder* and always will be, whether he's Amish or not." Sarah turned off the water, leaving the spuds to drain.

Mrs. Pratt wrapped the block of cheese she had been grating and wiped her hands. "We're done in here. You come with me, young lady. You're about to learn the wonders of MapQuest. Do you have that address with you?"

"*Jah*, it's in my purse." Sarah felt a seed of hope take root and begin to grow.

"Get it and meet me in my office."

Sarah had watched Mrs. Pratt work at the computer before with its flashing colors and music in the background, but never with so much at stake. She placed the tattered envelope on the desk.

Mrs. Pratt stared at the return address over her half-moon glasses, and then she began tapping on the keyboard. "Okay, are you ready to see something amazing?" she asked with a grin.

Sarah pulled up a hassock and sat down. "As much as I ever will be."

With a click of the mouse, suddenly the screen changed to a map. A large body of water marked the northern boundary of Cleveland, while a red arrow pointed to a spot on Davenport Drive. "That's where your brother lived when this letter was mailed." Mrs. Pratt picked up the envelope to peruse, while Sarah peered at the monitor. A complex grid of streets and highways offered no help whatsoever. Caleb might as well be living on the moon. She wrinkled her nose. "People locate each other using these things?"

"Just watch this." Mrs. Pratt clicked the mouse three more times, and with each subsequent tap the display changed to one with greater detail. The final screen revealed a neighborhood with the names of side streets clearly marked. Sarah reached out an index finger to touch the home of her brother...at least where he had lived three years ago. "Oh, my," she murmured.

"And if we wanted to jump in my car and visit Caleb? Just watch this." Mrs. Pratt typed the address for Country Pleasures B and B into one box and Caleb's address in the other. With another click of the mouse, numbered directions popped up, with left and right turns clearly marked.

"That is remarkable," Sarah said without taking her eyes from the monitor.

"Yep. I'll print copies of these maps and directions so you can show your parents." The copy machine behind them whirred to life, and moments later pieces of paper began falling into the tray.

"No, these are just for me, Mrs. Pratt. I don't want to get *mamm's* hopes up. Caleb may no longer live anywhere near here." She pointed to the spot denoting 885 Davenport Street, Cleveland, Ohio.

"If you decide to write him a letter and he writes back, you could look at these maps and find his neighborhood. Let me show you one more screen." She typed in new commands, and soon the northern half of the state of Ohio blossomed before their eyes. Again, large blue Lake Erie offered a northern reference point.

"Here we are in Fredericksburg." Mrs. Pratt held one finger on the spot. "And here is Davenport Street." She pointed with her other hand. "We live in Wayne County, and your brother lives in Cuyahoga County. Now you have an idea where Cleveland is in relation to us. Not that far away, relatively speaking, when you consider that half my family lives in Baton Rouge and the other half in northern Virginia."

On impulse, Sarah threw her arms around Mrs. Pratt and squeezed. "*Danki.* You have no idea how much this means to me."

The woman hugged her in return and kissed the top of her *kapp.* "You're welcome, but now I want you to run home. I have things covered here, and your mother might need you. Thanks for your help with tonight's dinner."

Sarah tucked the papers into her purse, shrugged on her coat, and stepped out into lightly falling snow. She filled her lungs with clean air and prayed halfway home.

Thank You, Lord, for leading me to my bruder. *Please watch over Caleb and guide his path. Keep him safe over Christmas and during the coming new year. And if it be Your will, help me find him.* With her prayer on its way, Sarah cleared her mind of useless thoughts and waited for God to speak to her.

As the front porch and twin chimneys of her beloved home came into view, she was blessed with intuition and made her decision. If she was to become Adam's wife and have *kinner* of her own someday, she needed to know why Caleb left home.

What is so important in Cleveland worth breaking mamm's *heart?*

NINE

Saturday

Does a mother ever know what goes on in the minds of her children? Sarah had always been the one Elizabeth thought would give her the least amount of trouble. Rebekah could be wily, with her mind spinning with ways to cut corners or pass off chores. And Katie could be downright dangerous at times. She'd been climbing trees, swinging on ropes from the loft window, and shimmying onto the backs of animals since she was a toddler. Elizabeth could never lay her on a quilt in the summer shade and take a catnap beside her. Off Katie would crawl to investigate the wonders of the pump house or the chicken coop.

But Sarah? That girl had been as predictable as robins in the spring. Shy, soft-spoken, and easily pleased, Sarah stayed where she was put, never sassed, and usually confided every hope or fear to her mother...until lately. Elizabeth knew that change comes to all women. They leave childhood and step into the adult world without a firm understanding of what they want or what's expected of them, yet she had always felt confident that steadfast Sarah would set a good example for her younger, more impetuous sisters.

So Elizabeth was uncomfortable when apprehension tickled the back of her mind.

For the past few days, Sarah had been dreamy and secretive, spending time holed up in her room when she wasn't at the inn. Tomorrow was the Lord's day. There would be no work at the B and B. All her *kinner* would be home, but Elizabeth chose not to wait for an overdue conversation. With a sigh she set down her sewing and climbed the stairs to her daughters' room.

"Sarah?" she called, knocking firmly. "I'd like a word with you."

After a moment the door swung wide, and a chilling sight greeted Elizabeth. Across Sarah's narrow bed lay every garment of clothing she owned. Dresses, skirts, aprons, *kapps*, socks, and underclothes had been scattered. Some of the items Sarah had outgrown and should have been handed down to Rebekah. Little bottles of lotion and shampoo sat in a heap next to her brush, comb, and toothbrush.

"Going on a trip?" Elizabeth asked, expecting a logical explanation, such as closet cleaning or drawer reorganization.

The girl glanced up with her honey brown eyes shining. "*Jah.* Do you know where the small suitcase is, *mamm*? The one I used when we traveled to Pennsylvania for cousin Susan's wedding a couple years ago? I've looked everywhere!" She shut her bottom drawer with a toe.

"It's up in the attic with the rest of them. Where do you think you're going?" Elizabeth closed the bedroom door, not wishing their conversation to be overheard.

Sarah, the child without an ounce of drama, calmly replied, "Cleveland," and then began folding her strewn blouses.

"Cleveland? What in the world for?" asked Elizabeth, but deep in her heart she knew.

"I'm going to find my brother. I wish to speak with him." Sarah didn't look at her mother as she smoothed wrinkles from her longest winter skirt.

"You're not making any sense, daughter. Nobody knows where he is."

"I know where he lives." The girl looked up and met Elizabeth's eye with the assurance of a ninety-year-old sage. "Albert Sidley gave me his most recent address."

Albert Sidley—Caleb's old pal from their days of softball and riding horses up into the hills? Elizabeth hadn't thought of that boy in a long time. Suddenly her knees felt weak, and she sat down hard on Rebekah's neatly made bed. "Your *bruder* wrote to Albert?" she asked hoarsely.

"*Jah,* a couple times." Sarah filled a plastic bag with her toiletries. "I don't mean to upset you, *mamm,* but I have a few questions for Caleb."

"What kinds of questions? After all these years, what could he possibly tell you that would be this important? He chose to leave us, Sarah. It was his decision to leave the Order and become English."

Sarah stopped organizing her small wardrobe. "Are you forbidding me from going? I'm nineteen years old—an adult, not a child. I've saved my own money. And these are my years to sample the English world before making up my mind."

Elizabeth thought she might be sick as her stomach took a nasty churn. Maybe she shouldn't have spread the hot pepper relish so generously on her sandwich. "So you've decided to take a *Rumschpringe* after all? Is this why you haven't taken classes in preparation of baptism? Is this why you've been dancing Adam Troyer around like a puppet on a string—changing the subject each time he brings up your wedding?"

Anger flashed in Sarah eyes. "I see Rebekah has been gossiping about me." She crossed her arms over her chest.

Elizabeth knew she walked a narrow precipice. "I'm not forbidding your trip to Cleveland, Sarah. It's your right, I suppose, but I am asking you to be practical. Cleveland isn't like downtown Fredericksburg, where you can hike to one end and back during a church bathroom break. It's huge with hundreds of thousands of people. Every big city has hidden dangers you know nothing about."

With agonizing slowness Sarah pulled several folded papers from her purse and set them on the bed. Elizabeth didn't need to ask what they were. "Did you get those at the fancy inn where you work?"

"*Jah*. I've been studying the maps for two days. I've practically memorized them. I'm sure I can find my way to Caleb's house. I've traced my path a hundred times."

"Your path?" Elizabeth felt every protective instinct in her body sharpen to full alert. "This is not the same thing as taking the back path to Josie's around the abandoned mill. Cleveland is far away for an Amish gal with no car."

After selecting one of the papers, Sarah sat down next to her mother and placed the sheet between them. "Here's where we are," she said, pointing with a finger. "And here is Cleveland." She tapped a spot on the map. "It's sixty-six and one-half miles." She spoke like a schoolteacher addressing her students.

"Is that right?" Elizabeth took hold of Sarah's chin and turned her face. "Are you going to walk those sixty-six and one-half miles in the middle of winter or hitch your horse to the buggy and pray for no blizzard?" She spoke without a hint of sarcasm. Somehow she needed to get through to her sweet, malleable child who had recently changed into a stubborn mule. "Those aren't country

71

roads with a buggy lane. They are crowded highways and inter-state freeways where cars and trucks travel at high speed."

Sarah smiled patiently as though Elizabeth were the thick-headed one. "Of course not. I can't drive a buggy to Cleveland, *mamm*. I know that. I plan to pay Mrs. Pratt for a ride to Canton, where I'll catch a bus. They have a route straight to downtown Cleveland with only one short stop in Akron." She patted Elizabeth's arm.

Elizabeth's heart stopped pumping blood for a moment. Her daughter had given this matter serious thought. "And what will one skinny Amish girl do in downtown Cleveland alone?" She rose and started pacing in the small room.

Sarah maintained her calm, cool composure. "Not to worry. I have several other maps, each more detailed than this one, and I've studied them as well. They have a good bus system besides a Rapid Transit train that stops close to Caleb's address." She patted the pile of clothes waiting for the suitcase. "I shall probably stay one night—two at the most—in case he wants to show me some sights. And I'll be home in plenty of time for Christmas."

"This notion is really stuck in your head, isn't it?" Elizabeth stopped pacing from the door to the window. "Have you given any thought to your *bruder*'s reaction to you showing up on his doorstep after five years? What if he doesn't want to talk to you? He might shut the door in your face." She would pray for forgiveness for her unkindness tonight, but as a mother she was desperate.

Sarah didn't seem offended. "I've thought about that, but I decided that since he's my brother, he'll talk to me. I only want a short time with him. I don't plan to move in or talk him into coming back to Wayne County. He might even be happy to see me. He always called me his *bleed madchen*."

The *Deutsch* name for "bashful girl" brought back painful memories. Elizabeth could hear Caleb's voice calling to his siblings as though it were yesterday. Caleb had been very fond of Sarah while growing up. Elizabeth steadied her nerves with several deep calming breaths. "If you are so stuck on this harebrained idea, then your father or I will go with you. That way you won't be alone." Having reached the only possible solution, she sighed with relief.

"No, *mamm*," said Sarah. "Neither you nor *daed* may come with me. It won't work then. You could spoil everything."

"What will spoil, Sarah? What's going on in that head of yours?"

"I have some questions for him, things I need to know before committing myself to God and the church, and certainly before committing to Adam Troyer in marriage. If you're there, Caleb might not tell me the truth." Her tone encouraged no further discussion on the subject.

Elizabeth stared at her eldest daughter almost without recognition. "I see. And when do you plan to leave on this trip?"

"On Monday. Business is slow at the inn earlier in the week. I'll have no trouble getting a few days off work. Now, if you'll excuse me, *mamm*, I'd like to go up to the attic and look for that suitcase before it grows dark." Sarah stepped around her mother and hurried from the room.

Elizabeth stood listening to overhead footsteps for a few moments before returning to the kitchen, feeling as though she'd been kicked by a mule. She poured a cup of cold coffee, slumped into a chair, and tried to think. Yet after ten minutes, still no insight occurred as to how she should handle the situation. Instead, memories of her son's tumultuous *Rumschpringe* flooded back, bringing shame and regret.

That summer had been the hottest in fifteen years. Temperatures soared into the nineties during the day and dropped little at night due to the oppressive humidity. Caleb had been working on a construction project in Wilmot—adding a hotel and conference center to a tourist restaurant and gift shop. Although most of the carpenters and roofers were Amish, the plumbers and electricians were English. Caleb had made new friends among them. Eli gave him plenty of leeway to mingle because Caleb hadn't joined the church yet. But when he started staying after work and missing supper several nights a week, Eli went to the barn for a father-son chat. Eli, who almost never raised his voice, lost his temper when he watched his son stumble from the buggy smelling of beer.

"Drunkenness is an abomination before the Lord," Eli shouted.

"Who's drunk? I had a couple beers after work, that's all," Caleb shouted back. But his glassy eyes and the slur of his words had fooled no one.

Afterward, there had been no further verbal confrontations, but both men grew more edgy and sullen as the interminable summer wore on. When the crews completed the rough framing on the hotel, highly skilled Caleb stayed until early fall to build interior walls, floors, and doorways. The family seldom saw him during these months because he went to work with an *Englischer*. He left the house early and came home late, sneaking into his room and barely speaking to his parents and sisters.

One Saturday night Eli spotted sparks shooting into the sky from a fire down by the creek. Amish youths often hosted bonfire parties to roast hot dogs and marshmallows as cooler evenings spurred social events. But there were no buggies parked in the yard, only five or six pickup trucks. Loud music poured from a boom box, while shouts and laughter could be heard all the way to the house.

Tossing and turning in his damp bed sheets, unable to sleep, Eli had had enough. He dressed and walked down to the creek to turn down the music. No one had noticed the long-bearded Amish father near the picnic table until Caleb and one of his friends decided to refill their quart-sized cups. Then they discovered that someone had drained the keg of beer into the tall grass of the meadow.

The young men soon wandered back to their trucks and went home.

Caleb soon left for Cleveland on a construction project… and never returned.

Elizabeth felt her hands turn clammy as her chest grew tight. She couldn't bear to lose another child to the big city and English ways. When no better idea came to mind, she took pen and paper to jot a hurried message, folding the paper over twice when she finished.

"Katie!" she called. When the girl appeared in the doorway, Elizabeth commanded, "Take this to the Troyer farm and be quick about it. Give this note to no one but Adam. And do not let curiosity get the better of you. It's not your concern."

With a nod of her head, her youngest girl flew off. Elizabeth sat praying she hadn't made another huge mistake.

TEN

Sunday

Sarah rechecked her suitcase for necessities and her purse for money and directions for the tenth time. For once she was grateful it had snowed the previous night. Usually her family traveled to another district for church services on their district's off week, but with several inches of new snow and more on the way, the Beachys were staying home today. And she had plenty to do yet if she was to leave tomorrow morning. At least Mrs. Pratt agreed to drive her to the bus station, although she too had tried to convince her to wait until spring.

Spring would be too late. Adam would never give her that much time. He was patient and kind with kids and animals, but he could be stubborn once he'd fixed his sights on something.

Her mother, on the other hand, had surprised her. Sarah had half expected *mamm* to forbid the trip or at least demand that one parent accompany her, but she had done neither. Maybe her mother realized she was an adult, fully capable of traveling alone and making important decisions about her life.

Setting aside her purse with a sigh, Sarah headed downstairs to help fix lunch before her mother hollered up the steps again. She entered the kitchen with a cheery *"Guder nachmittag."*

Katie and Rebekah both returned the greeting, while Elizabeth merely grunted acknowledgement that someone had spoken.

"What are we having for lunch?" asked Sarah.

Elizabeth pursed her lips and then pointed at the table, where a loaf of freshly baked bread, jars of pickled vegetables, and a cold meatloaf waited to be served. She took a bowl of pasta salad out of the refrigerator that had been fixed yesterday.

"Ah, good, meatloaf sandwiches. One of my favorites. I'll slice a tomato and break off some lettuce leaves."

"You're not too busy to eat with us?" Elizabeth asked in a chilly voice.

Sarah's head snapped around. Never before could she remember her mother being snide. She might not be forbidding the trip, but she certainly wasn't happy about it. "I have plenty of time. I'm not leaving until tomorrow morning. Mrs. Pratt will take me to the station at eight o'clock."

"Where's Sarah going?" asked the younger girls in perfect unison.

"Never you mind where she's going." Elizabeth set the bowl on the table with a thud. "Katie, slice the bread and don't make the slices too thick. Rebekah, cut that meatloaf in one-inch pieces. I hear your father in the mudroom."

A moment later Sarah expected to see the rosy cheeks of her *daed*, but instead Adam Troyer walked into the kitchen, rubbing his hands together to warm them up.

"Adam," said Sarah, not hiding her shock.

"*Jah*, it's me. Glad my face is still familiar." He winked with a broad smile. "The snow is sure giving us a run for the money this year, no?"

"True, 'tis early. Usually it holds off till after Christmas." Sarah stood holding a tomato in the palm of her hand like a prize. The other three females glanced between Sarah and Adam as though expecting something to happen.

"*Ach*, I see you're ready for lunch. Sorry about my bad timing, Mrs. Beachy." Adam twirled his hat brim between his fingers.

"Nonsense. It's a simple meal and we have plenty. Pull up a chair."

Adam did as directed as Eli trailed in, looking flushed from his morning chores. After silent prayers, Sarah tried to catch Adam's eye to no avail. He had created an enormous sandwich and was eating with complete concentration.

Sarah smelled something fishy, despite the meatloaf filling. She ate half her sandwich trying to figure out the reason for his impromptu visit. He couldn't know about her bus trip. She'd only recently decided to go.

Conversation around the table centered on the upcoming school play. But at the first lull, Elizabeth asked, "No appetite, daughter? Everyone else appears to like my meatloaf."

"It's delicious, but I'll save the other half to finish later," Sarah said, as Adam attacked a mound of macaroni salad like a man many days without a meal.

When he'd finished, he looked Sarah in the eye. "How about walking me to my buggy? My *mamm* sent some cheese streusels, and I forgot to bring them in."

"First I must help with dishes," she said, rising to her feet.

"No," Elizabeth commanded. "You go with Adam. Your sisters will clean up. Maybe he can talk some sense into you since I couldn't."

Eli grunted—apparently the Beachy family reply of the day—and headed for the front room. Her sisters exchanged confused glances but kept silent. Sarah slipped on her cloak and followed

Adam outside. Once they had reached his buggy she asked, "Did my mother invite you here today?"

He turned his sky blue eyes toward her. "*Jah*, she sent me a note. She's very worried about you. She doesn't understand your sudden urge to find your *bruder*, and I sure don't, either. What's going on with you?"

She pulled her hands up into her sleeves. "I don't know really. I just want to find Caleb and make sure he's all right. Nobody has heard from him in a long time. That doesn't mean all's well and good in the English city."

Adam stepped up into his buggy and offered her his hand. When she'd settled next to him, he covered her knees with a wool blanket. "Okay, but this isn't the best weather for traveling. Why don't you wait until sometime next summer?"

"I need to go now, Adam. You want us to get married and become a family, but I look at dear Mrs. Pratt and see such loneliness in her life since her kids moved away. It upsets me."

He scratched his jaw. "What does an English woman have to do with us?"

"Plenty. I've noticed that same unhappiness in my mother's face too whenever someone mentions Caleb's name. She still misses him, especially this time of year."

"Not everybody born Amish stays that way. You know that. Caleb chose to leave, but again, I don't see what that has to do with us getting hitched." He reached for her hand under the lap robe.

"*Kinner* might be nothing but a source of heartache for a woman," she murmured. "I have some thinking to do before I marry, Adam. I want to know why Caleb didn't want to stay Amish. How could he so easily leave the people who loved him? He owns a car. He could come home for a visit, but he never has." Sarah heard anger in her voice and didn't like it. *Why take my frustrations with Caleb out on Adam? He has every right to be curious about my plans.*

He rubbed the back of his neck. "All right, Sarah. I told your mother I'd *try* to talk you out of this, but I didn't promise I would. Because you're set on this idea, I won't stop you, but I'm going along to make sure you get there and back safely."

Sarah pulled back her hand and turned on the seat. "Why would you do that? I'm leaving tomorrow, and you have to work."

"I'm coming because I care about you. Besides, I still have vacation time left."

She felt a disjointed uneasiness. She didn't want Adam to accompany her. If Caleb agreed to talk, he certainly wouldn't do so in front of someone who was a virtual stranger. Besides, once she had determined a course of action, she looked forward to going alone. "No, *danki.* I'll be fine. You shouldn't use up all your vacation days. Your *daed* will need your help with spring planting."

Adam exhaled through his teeth in frustration. "Don't worry about springtime. You're not thinking straight. A bus terminal is no place for a woman. Someone might try to talk to you."

"If somebody tries to get too friendly, I'll tell him to be on his way. I'm not a child who hides behind her mama's skirt."

"No, you're a pigheaded woman who won't listen to reason." His nostrils flared.

Sarah didn't appreciate his overbearing attitude. They weren't married yet. She had a right to make her own decisions at this point. She clenched her teeth. "Caleb will be more receptive if only his sister visits. I'm going alone, Adam. My mind is made up. Now I'm taking my *pighead* and the rest of me indoors. It's too cold out here to argue about this anymore." She threw off the blanket and jumped down from the buggy.

Adam muttered something she was glad she didn't catch; then he followed after her. "Wait, Sarah. Give me one more minute."

She turned, summoning every ounce of patience she had.

"Are you certain you're going to the right house? What address do you have for him?"

"Eight-eighty-five Davenport Street," she repeated from memory. She'd studied the MapQuest search results until her eyes had crossed.

Adam nodded slowly. "*Jah*, that's his most recent address."

Sarah, already halfway back to the house, froze in midstep. She turned again and stared at Adam with eyes as round as saucers. "How could you possibly know that?"

He shuffled his boots in the driveway. "I asked around at work a couple years ago. The brother of one of the men Cal left town with works at my plant. He gave me the address for safekeeping."

"For *safekeeping*? You knew where my *bruder* was all this time and didn't say anything?" She huffed out air like a goat preparing to charge a stranger in its pasture.

"It was for your own good, Sarah." Adam had taken on a goat-like appearance.

"*I'll* decide what's good for me and what's not, Adam Troyer, thank you very much. I'll see you when I return from Cleveland." She stomped up the steps and slammed the door with more energy than necessary.

Fortunately, the kitchen was empty of Beachys. And by the time Sarah reached her bedroom, her anger had cooled and been replaced with regret and shame for losing her temper. She lifted her window sash to call down a hasty apology.

But Adam and his buggy were gone.

At eight o'clock the next morning, Sarah stood with suitcase in hand at the back door of Country Pleasures. She'd put on her warmest clothes, kissed her two sleeping sisters, and crept downstairs quietly but discovered the kitchen empty. No hug goodbye from her *mamm* or last-minute warnings. However, her mother had left a brown bag bearing her name in red letters on the table. Inside, Sarah found two sandwiches, two apples, a granola bar, chips, and a bottle of water. *Mamm must fear Cleveland has no food,* she thought, but she tucked the sack into her tote bag with appreciation. After a hearty bowl of cereal, she headed for the B and B.

Mrs. Pratt chatted in good spirits on the drive to Canton. "Now, you be sure to see Lake Erie. It'll look like the ocean—you can't see across it."

Sarah had never seen an ocean to compare the lake to, but she smiled politely.

"Make your brother take you to the zoo—it's one of the best in the country. Don't miss a single exhibit. And make sure you go to the West Side Market—so many good things to sample before you buy. You'll feel right at home."

"I'll try to remember, but I'm not sure how much sightseeing time we'll have. I'm only staying a day or two."

"He might want to take you on a whirlwind tour. And those three places shouldn't be missed." Mrs. Pratt glanced at her. "The Cleveland Museum of Art is also spectacular, but I don't expect that would be your cup of tea."

Sarah looked at her dear friend, and the two women burst out laughing. "I don't imagine, but I'll keep it fourth on my list." Sarah settled back to watch the passing scenery at sixty miles an hour. Excitement and anticipation replaced the anxiety and fear instilled by her *mamm* and beau. This would be her grand adventure—something to look back on when she rocked on the front porch, bouncing a grandbaby on her knee. She could tell her granddaughters how she'd traveled alone to Cleveland to find their great-uncle just like a private detective.

When they arrived at the bus station, Mrs. Pratt pulled into the drop-off zone. "Should I park and wait with you until it's time for the bus to leave?"

"No, *danki*. You've already done enough by buying my ticket online and driving me here. I understand where to pick up the ticket, so please don't worry. I'm not the least bit nervous." Sarah grinned as joy swelled in her veins like a tonic.

"Wonderful! I hope you have a smashing good time, but I want you to take something as a favor to me." Mrs. Pratt pulled a cell phone from her coat pocket.

"You know our bishop doesn't allow—"

"It's for emergency use only. Your bishop won't have a problem if someone uses a phone in an emergency. Most likely you won't need it, and it'll stay unused at the bottom of your purse. But in the off chance you land in hot water, you'll be able to call me. I can jump in my car and be anywhere in Cleveland within three hours." She lifted one eyebrow, and when Sarah didn't respond, she hit the automatic door button. All locks clicked into position simultaneously. "I won't let you out until you agree."

The woman didn't sound as though she were joking. Sarah shook her head, and then she leaned over to hug her employer. "*Danki*, Mrs. Pratt. I'll take it along, just in case."

"I have the number of the inn already programmed into it. All you do is hit this green button twice to make the home phone ring. If you get my voice mail, leave your name and I'll call you right back."

Sarah briefly studied the cell phone before tucking it into her purse. After another hug, she hopped out of the van and walked into the bus station, feeling more exuberant than at any point in her nineteen years of life.

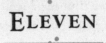

Eleven

Monday

Cal Beachy rubbed a clear patch on his steamy window and stared out at the bleak street scene below. All the pristine white snow had turned to dirty gray slush that sprayed the sidewalk with each passing vehicle. Walkers had to be careful because the sidewalks ran close to the sloppy streets. He, however, had no place to go. Even though he'd spent the last week at the union hall, his one job opportunity had fizzled out.

Work would soon begin on a new library wing, but the contractor who had been awarded the carpentry bid hadn't hired Cal. His prospects looked grim until the spring, when more construction projects would start. His friend Pete Taylor had faithfully dropped him off every morning at the hall until his new job had started. Then Cal rode public transportation downtown, but today he chose to save the Rapid Transit fare.

Cal was concentrating so intently on a fender bender that caught his attention that he didn't hear the knock until the pounding grew insistent. When he pulled open the door, in marched Pete carrying a large box and grocery sack. "Man, you need to get your hearing checked. I've been standing out there for five minutes."

"Sorry, I was watching the excitement on the street. Did you cause the accident and slip clean away?" teased Cal.

Pete grinned. "Nah, it was two chicks talking on their cell phones. Need I say more?" He shrugged off his jacket and threw it on the couch. "I brought a double pepperoni, extra cheese so we can celebrate. And I bought both Coke and beer—what's your drinking pleasure?" He pulled two six-packs from the bag and held them aloft.

"Give me a Coke. Beer makes me say stupid things." Cal pulled a can loose and popped the top. "What exactly are we celebrating?"

Pete opened a Coke too and took a long swallow. "You finally joining the world of the employed, of course." He wiped his mouth on his sleeve.

"Then you might want to take back the pizza. I didn't get the job."

Pete looked flabbergasted. "You're kidding. I talked to the construction manager myself. I worked for him a while ago on several projects. Because I'd already signed elsewhere, he asked me for recommendations. Your name topped my short list."

Cal helped himself to a slice of pizza. Though undeserving of celebration, he hadn't eaten since yesterday. "Yeah, I went to the interview with the guy, but he said the library branch was out in Mentor. I asked him where that was." Cal devoured the slice before continuing the story. "He explained and then asked if getting to the job site might pose a problem." He looked up at Pete who stared back, flummoxed.

"And? What did you say?"

"I said right now I didn't own a car, but that I planned to pick up a used one. I would take the Rapid Transit until then."

Pete stared at Cal for a moment and then drained the contents of the can. After a manly belch, he sat down at the table across from his friend. "Is that when the interview came screeching to a halt?"

"Pretty much," said Cal, eyeing the pizza. The first slice barely scratched the surface of his hunger.

Pete pushed the box closer. "Go ahead, eat. That's why I bought it." He leaned his head back against the wall, deep in thought. "First of all, the Rapid doesn't run along the lake to Mentor. It takes an inland, eastern route. Secondly, you should *never* admit you don't have transportation to a job site. You should have said, 'I'll have no problem getting to work' and left it at that. Then you would have had several days to buy or borrow a car, or arrange some way to get there."

"That's what I'd planned to do, but I didn't want to lie and say I had a car when I didn't."

Pete shook his head vigorously. "No, but instead you sounded unreliable. You still don't get it, Cal. *Englischers*, as you used to call them, throw out a line of bull to get what they want in this world. Once your foot is in the door, then you can scramble around to make it happen."

"Sounds like lying to me."

"It's more like telling a future truth."

Cal sighed wearily and finished his pizza, although the second slice didn't taste half as good as the first. "I get what you mean. I'll keep that in mind the next time around."

Pete didn't hide his skepticism regarding the likelihood of a next time. "You want another?" he asked, opening a second Coke. "If not, I'll stick these in the fridge." After Cal shook his head, Pete sauntered into the kitchen with the two six packs. "P.U.," he called. "Did something crawl in here and die?" He walked back holding his nose.

Cal tossed down his pizza crust. "What are you talking about?"

"You didn't go squirrel hunting in the park and stash the bodies in your refrigerator, did you? Because this ain't Fredericksburg. Discharging firearms within city limits is strictly illegal."

Cal smirked until he noticed Pete's earnest face. "No, I didn't shoot anything. I have no idea what smells funny, but there are no dead animals in my kitchen. And I didn't bring any guns when I moved here."

Pete relaxed back in his chair. "Whew, that's a relief. You might want to check out what's past its prime, but wait until after I leave." He pulled a large piece from the box.

"Thanks for the pizza, by the way," said Cal, recalling his manners.

"No problem. Remember when we were roommates? We ate pizza five times a week. Four men sharing an apartment, and not one of us could cook. Why couldn't one guy have been a Wolfgang Puck wannabe?" He folded his pizza slice in half before taking a bite.

Cal figured Mr. Puck must be a famous chef and smiled as bittersweet memories of his first year in Cleveland came back. How he'd loved that loft apartment with its twelve-foot ceilings, three bedrooms, two bathrooms, and a view of Lake Erie. The four roommates had rotated months as to who slept on the couch and who had their own room, but even the couch had been comfortable. A man could fall asleep hearing foghorns from passing ships and the mournful whistle of trains as they slowed to cross the bridges into downtown. The apartment had been close to everything—stores, restaurants, clubs, parks, and sport stadiums. He'd earned good money back then, and he had treated pals to football and baseball games. At first he'd been shocked by the price of a hot dog during those events—twice the cost of an entire package at the grocery store. But in time he became accustomed to overpricing. He called it the excitement factor—the more fun you had, the more you had to pay for food and drinks.

He and his three English friends had gotten along well. Everyone pitched in to keep the place fairly tidy. On Sunday afternoons they would sit in front of the big screen hooting, hollering, and throwing foam footballs at the TV. Then Pete moved in with his girlfriend, and they had set a spring wedding date. Keeping up with a third of the rent and utilities was beyond his reach when Cal was laid off, so he'd moved into this third-floor walkup sight unseen...and he had hated the cramped, dismal rooms ever since.

Pete reached for more pizza. "We had some good times, old buddy."

"Yeah, we did," agreed Cal. "How are the weddin' plans coming along?"

Pete laughed. "Growing in leaps and bounds. At last count Michelle has invited eight bridesmaids and changed the ceremony from our neighborhood church to the huge cathedral downtown. But as long as she's happy, I don't mind."

Cal felt a stab of jealousy but tamped it down quickly. He had holed up like an urban hermit instead of trying to meet women. "You're a lucky man," he said, finishing his Coke.

"That I am. Things will turn around for you too. I hear rumblings in the industry that companies might start hiring after the first of the year to be ready for spring ground breaking. Have your resume in hand, prepared to interview. Your chance will come, and then you can move out of this place." Pete stood abruptly. "I gotta take off. Michelle is cooking steaks tonight, and she doesn't like to keep them warm. The rest of the pizza is yours."

With that, Pete picked up his coat and hurried out the door, leaving Cal alone once again. Strong odors of garlic and onion seeped through the walls from the apartment next door. Folks sure cooked some odd food in this neighborhood. He padded into the kitchen and opened the refrigerator door to assess what had offended Pete's senses. Nothing smelled out of the ordinary as he ruffled through old take-out containers, discovering a container of Chinese he'd forgotten about. He popped the lid to evaluate the remnants. Although it appeared different from the original condition, it didn't seem disgusting. He hadn't a clue how long food could safely be kept. Growing up in a family of six guaranteed no leftovers went uneaten. His mother scraped anything not consumed by lunchtime the next day into the slop bucket on the porch. Their sow promptly polished off the bucket's contents without complaint.

Cal ate a hearty forkful of the egg fu yong and then another. After all, he'd been raised to believe wasting food was sinful. By his fourth forkful, a dull ache began in his gut and then spread upward into his chest. Cal barely reached the bathroom before the spoiled takeout, spicy pizza, and carbonated soda made a hasty reappearance. Filled with shame and revulsion, he scrubbed his mouth with his toothbrush and then began systematically cleaning out his fridge of suspicious meals. Out went partial cans of Coke, green-tinged bread, hard-as-rock dinner rolls, and a bag of shriveled apples he'd bought at the outdoor market. He tossed the eggs and milk into the garbage bag without bothering to sniff, his stomach still churning from the previous onslaught. Then he scrubbed out the appliance's interior with bleach water.

Wouldn't mamm *be surprised to see me on my hands and knees, cleaning?* Another thought struck him. *Wouldn't she be ashamed at how low I've sunk into despair?*

Being out of work and broke were states many men found themselves in at some point in life, but behaving woefully was another matter. Cal let days go by without bothering to shave, shower, or to put on clean clothes. A person without a job should have plenty of time to take care of himself and sweep the floor and dust his apartment.

He rose to his feet, tied the garbage bag shut, and headed down the steps to the alley. After ridding his home of rotten food, he vowed to pull himself together. He had sunk just about as low as a man could go. Considering the food he'd last consumed, he would have to look up to see bottom.

Pete had said things in the construction industry might turn around in the spring. Cal sure hoped that was true, because gazing in the mirror was becoming harder to do. Before climbing the stairs to his apartment, he remembered to check his mailbox in the front hallway. He unlocked the metal cubicle and pulled out flyers and a few bills. When one official-looking letter caught his eye, he lowered himself to the dusty steps to open the envelope. He was among the minority collecting unemployment benefits without access to a computer. The bureau mailed out his biweekly checks promptly; however, other communications were often delayed by processing. Cal scanned the sheet, hoping for an extension of benefits or an increase in the amount. Neither was forthcoming.

Just when he thought life couldn't get any worse, the devil stepped in to illustrate how foolishly he had been thinking. His benefits, barely adequate to pay rent and keep the utilities connected, were about to run out. He had exhausted his share of the pie designed to bridge the gap between his former job and the next.

He should have looked harder for work.

He should have shown up at the union hall regularly.

Because as grim as his housing situation was, it sure beat living in a cardboard box under the Memorial Shoreway Bridge.

TWELVE

Sarah squirmed and fidgeted during the entire bus ride from Canton to Cleveland, unable to read her book or nap. She nibbled a sandwich *mamm* had packed, grateful for her foresight. And she had time to think long and hard about her mother, Mrs. Pratt, and Adam. An Amish girl was expected to marry, and if God was willing, bear children. If she possessed so many doubts now, maybe she wasn't cut out for a woman's noblest calling.

As houses, factories, and endless commercial strips passed beyond her window, the one person she didn't dwell on was Caleb Beachy.

Best to leave meeting him in God's hands.

She couldn't turn back now as the bus pulled into the Greyhound station's parking lot. After retrieving her bag, she headed inside and found the snack bar, ticket counter, and ladies' room in the airy terminal. Her grand adventure had begun. People waiting to board buses or looking for anticipated loved ones eyed her curiously as she gazed around the room. She doubted they saw many Amish folk in Cleveland, especially not a single woman traveling alone.

A kind-looking woman at the information counter smiled as Sarah approached. "May I help you?" she asked, perusing her clothing. "Where did you come from, miss?"

"Fredericksburg," Sarah answered cheerily.

"Virginia? I have a sister living in Richmond."

"No, Fredericksburg, Ohio." Upon the woman's perplexed expression, she added, "It's a small town south of Wooster."

"I see, but actually I should be asking where you're headed. Do you need to make a connection?"

Sarah withdrew one of the maps from her bag. "I wish to take the Rapid train to Davenport Street."

The woman scanned the sheet, locating the "X" Mrs. Pratt had marked before handing it back to her. "You need to take the Red Line and get off at the West Boulevard-Cudell stop. You can catch the train at Public Square. From here, you can either walk to the square or catch the Euclid Avenue connector." She pulled a pad from her desk drawer.

"I'll walk," said Sarah, unsure what a connector was.

"Okay, you're on Chester Avenue." The woman pointed toward the street. "Head west, which is to the right, until you get to East Ninth. Then turn right, go two blocks, turn left on Superior, and walk to Public Square. You can't miss it. The Rapid Transit station is the lowest level of the Terminal Tower." While she spoke, she marked on the pad with red marker. "When you get to the square, look up. The tallest building is the one you want. Good luck, honey." She ripped off the top sheet and handed it to Sarah.

She thanked the woman and left the station, clutching yet another map in her hand. Under the terminal's canopy she studied the red marks and breathed a sigh of relief—it was only a six-block walk.

But as she set out, the light snow steadily increased to near-blizzard conditions. By the time she reached Ninth Street, she couldn't see ten feet before her. Sidewalk shoveling had been spotty at best. Some storekeepers had cleared a path, but many abandoned storefronts promised a foot of slush to trudge through. By the time Sarah turned onto Superior Avenue, her outer bonnet and gloves were soggy, and the inside of her leather boots felt clammy.

However, she forgot how cold and damp she was the moment she arrived at Public Square. The festive display of holiday lights snatched her breath away. All four quadrants of the Square blazed with colorful blinking exhibits, one more impressive than the next. As she crossed the street, she entered a wonderland of red-and-green walkways winding through dozens of illuminated Christmas trees. Each glowed from hundreds of points of light. She marveled at the Soldiers and Sailors Monument and stood in awe before the Old Stone Church, beckoning people inside to worship. Even though most of the decorations were secular, Sarah spotted a Nativity scene in one quadrant that drew her like a moth to a flame.

As snowflakes fell on the ceramic sheep and wooden shepherds, she approached the manger with her heart swelling with anticipation.

Wise men journeyed for hundreds of miles two thousand years ago. Can't I walk a few blocks without complaining of discomfort?

Sarah stood transfixed for several minutes while office workers and shoppers hurried past her. She wasn't in a rush, though. She paused before the gentle reminder of what was possible through faith.

After a little while, she smiled and turned up her face to try to determine which building was the tallest, but heavy snow obliterated the skyline.

A young man wearing a stocking cap and baggy jeans paused beside her and stared up too. "Wha'cha looking for?"

"The Terminal Tower." She withdrew a damp map from her pocket.

"It's right in front of you," he answered, his grin revealing a gold tooth. "Cross the street and you're there." Before she could thank him, he disappeared into the throng.

Sarah fell in step with the people entering the building. The lobby's interior—marble floors and walls, a picture-frame ceiling of carved golden roses, brass latticework above each doorway—caused her mouth to drop open. Never had she seen anything so ornate. She trailed the crowd of tan trench coats, black briefcases, and plaid scarves into an inner court of shops and restaurants. *And English tourists think Amish folk dress alike.* All the stores seemed to sell only one type of item—fancy underwear, perfume, scented soaps and lotions, tennis shoes, jewelry—instead of a little of everything like back home. She walked to the railing and peered down into the Rapid Transit station two floors below. Heading for the escalator marked "To Trains," she almost followed the tide of humanity sheeplike onto the wrong train.

High on the wall hung "eastbound" and "westbound" maps with the stops along each route indicated. Sarah felt a surge of adrenaline when she spotted the West Boulevard-Cudell station on the Red Line—the stop nearest Davenport Street. *I'm getting close…that much closer to my* bruder.

"Can I help you, miss?"

Sarah turned to face a security guard. "I'd like to take the Red Line."

He nodded, walking her over to a machine. "Five dollars will buy an all-day pass. You can ride as much as you like. Just put your money in and press the All-Day button."

Sarah withdrew a five-dollar bill and studied the contraption, but she couldn't figure out where the money should go.

"Here, let me show you." The guard plucked the bill from her fingers.

She watched him insert it into the machine, press a button, and take the ticket that popped out.

"If you stay longer than twenty-four hours, these kiosks are at every station. Now watch how those people feed their tickets into the turnstile. And be sure to take the ticket with you when it comes back out."

Sarah ran to the Red Line turnstiles as though late for school with the guard close on her heels. He didn't leave her side until she emerged on the other side with her ticket in hand. "Listen for your stop," he called with hands cupped around his mouth.

She waved and grinned until her face hurt. When the train stopped at the platform, Sarah and the other commuters surged aboard like cattle into livestock trailers. Seats filled up quickly with the nimbler travelers, so she grasped a metal pole as they rattled out of the underground station. Soon the train careened back into daylight as she was jostled between other riders. She dipped her head for a glimpse of the city whenever the train rose higher than the deep valley it followed.

"West Boulevard-Cudell, next stop," announced the overhead speaker.

"That's my stop," she said to no one in particular.

"Better stand by the door so you're ready when it opens," advised a girl with dozens of skinny braids. She bobbed her head to the left.

"Thanks," Sarah said, moving into position. When the train lurched to a stop and the door opened, she jumped onto the platform, away from transportation that seemed to operate without human direction. Several people gave her odd looks as they climbed the stairs to street level. Under a streetlight, Sarah studied her map to regain her bearing. Only a few blocks separated her from Caleb's last known address. She strode off at a brisk pace as daylight slipped away. With the snowstorm and the year's shortest day in less than two weeks, darkness soon enveloped her in a neighborhood of boarded-up windows, sagging porches, and few shoveled sidewalks.

The cold pervaded her wool coat, thick socks, and ankle-length skirt. Her knit gloves and leather boots were no match for the slush tossed onto sidewalks from passing cars. Sarah's nose began to run as her spirits flagged.

What if Caleb doesn't want to see me? What if he shuts the door in my face? Or what if he no longer lives at his most recent address? That possibility had occurred to her back home, but she assumed new tenants would provide a current address. Now, walking the lonely streets and seeing few friendly faces, she realized the folly of her logic. A seed of fear began to grow in her empty belly. She'd eaten *mamm*'s sandwiches, potato chips, and fruit long ago. Where would she spend the night if Caleb no longer resided at 885 Davenport Street?

When she reached that address, she discovered a large brick apartment building instead of a house. Soot and grime had discolored the exterior, and the windowsills badly needed painting, but a ghost of its former glory still remained.

When a mother and child emerged through the front door, Sarah darted in before it closed behind them. A board of buttons hung on the wall, with names on cards beside each one. She looked at button after button until her focus landed on "C. Beachy, 314." Her breath caught in her throat. "*Danki*, Lord, that he hasn't moved again," she whispered.

Hesitantly, she pushed his button and waited. The interior door began to buzz jarringly. On impulse, she pulled the handle before the noise stopped. Ahead lay a narrow hallway with several doors, and on the right a wide staircase. She climbed the steps to the third floor feeling cold, tired, wet, hungry, and hopeful. She crept down a dingy hallway with carpeting that hadn't been cleaned in a decade, finally pausing at number 314. Would he even remember his *bleed madchen*? Would he be angry she had tracked him down?

Sarah knocked and waited. She lifted her hand to knock again when the metal door swung wide and her brother appeared in the doorway, holding a letter in his hand. He looked much thinner with short curly hair and a scruffy beard. But it was Caleb Beachy—his warm brown eyes fringed with thick lashes hadn't changed. "Caleb?" she asked softly.

"Sarah? Is that really you or am I dreaming?" He leaned against the doorjamb, gazing down on her.

"It's me. Mind if I come in? I'm freezing."

Cal straightened and moved back. "Sorry, come on in. You gave me quite a shock."

"I s'pose so." Sarah stepped past him into a cluttered apartment with dingy walls and worn carpet that smelled faintly sour.

"Don't mind the place. The cleaning lady called in sick this week." He grabbed a stack of newspapers from one end of the sofa.

She glanced up to make certain he was joking. "Most men aren't very tidy," she murmured, shrugging off her coat.

Cal looked alarmed when he reached for the garment. "This coat is soaking wet! You'll catch pneumonia if we don't get you warmed up." He pulled her over to a steam radiator, turned the valve fully open, and yanked off her soggy bonnet. Droplets of water flew in all directions. "Take off those boots while I get some dry socks," he ordered, laying her coat and hat across a chair to dry.

Ten minutes later, Sarah sat sipping black coffee in a huge sweat-shirt over her dress with thick socks up to her knees. Cal turned up the heat in the apartment until her teeth had stopped chattering.

"So, how do you like living in Cleveland?" She peered around the room, trying not to wrinkle her nose.

"I love it! There're so many things to do. Okay, this place isn't the best, but you should have seen my first apartment...beautiful! I'll be moving outta here as soon as construction picks up. Bad economy, dead of winter. You know how things are."

Actually, she didn't know. Work remained constant within her limited experience. "Why are there so many abandoned houses in your neighborhood?" she asked.

"The real estate bubble—people buying homes they couldn't afford to resell for quick profits. Then the bank financing dried up, and they were foreclosed on."

Sarah chewed her lip. "Why would they buy homes they couldn't pay for?"

"It's hard to explain. Instead, tell me how you got here." Cal refilled her coffee mug.

She recounted her trip on Greyhound and the Rapid Transit, including the incredible display on Public Square. "It looked very festive, but that many lights must cost a pretty penny in electricity. I saw plenty of better uses for the city's money, like sidewalk shoveling."

Cal scratched his ear. "Yeah, but the lights get folks in the mood for Christmas."

"Everybody was rushing by so fast, I think I was the only one who appreciated the Nativity scene."

"That's not true. People come downtown just to see the displays. Your ten-minute crowd assessment isn't fair."

"That's good to hear." *Annoying my* bruder *is not why I came.*

She rose from the couch and walked into the kitchen for milk to take the edge off the bitter coffee. But when she opened his refrigerator, a foul smell assailed her senses. "No milk, Cal?" she asked, trying not to gag.

"No. If I'd known about your visit, I would have gone shopping." Cal leaned around her to shut the door with his elbow.

Sarah faced him. "You have practically no food whatsoever. And I noticed you've lost weight." The emaciated state of both the apartment and her brother had set off alarms in her head. *How long has he been out of work?*

"I told you I hadn't gone grocery shopping."

She crossed her arms. "But I see you have a six-pack of beer in there."

Cal reared back. "I didn't buy that, Sarah. Why have you come—to criticize me or pass judgment on my life? I'm not Amish anymore, in case you haven't noticed."

Sarah walked back to the living room radiator. "Are you anything at all? I mean, do you attend church up here?" She attempted to sound conversational.

He exhaled through his teeth, exasperated. "No, little sister, I don't go to church. God seems to have forgotten me."

Time and silence spun out in the room. Then quietly she said, "Maybe it's you who have forgotten God."

Emotions of anger, sorrow, and finally resignation crossed his face in succession. "Whatever you say. Are you hungry? I have pizza that's still good. A friend brought it over today. Let's have it for supper."

"Jah, danki," she said, wondering if he'd heard her stomach rumbling.

Cal carried a pizza box, two Cokes, and paper napkins to a wobbly kitchen table.

Sarah ate two slices, trying not to pepper him with questions.

But Cal had his own questions once they finished eating. "What do you want? I know you came for a reason."

She blushed to the roots of her damp hair. "I want to know why you left Wayne County. It's important to me because I'm thinking of getting married and having kids someday."

He stared out the window at the falling snow and chose his words carefully. "It was all about money," he said. "I couldn't believe how much union carpenters got paid. They drove trucks loaded with every gadget and could eat in restaurants every single day. I thought I'd try life as an *Englischer* for a while...just to get it out of my system before I settled down. I always thought I'd come home after a year or two." He glanced at her with tired, dark-ringed eyes.

"So why didn't you, especially after the good-paying work dried up?" She reached for his hand, but he pulled away.

"Because things happen, Sarah, things you know nothing about. They have made going home impossible."

"Nothing should separate you from your family, not if—"

"Oh, really?" he interrupted. "And what do you think *daed* would say about this?" He rolled up his shirtsleeve to reveal a large colorful tattoo on his bicep. It was a heart entwined with snakes surrounding a woman's name.

She gasped involuntarily.

"That's not all. Once I got drunk on a Saturday night and woke up in a stranger's...home. And I've wasted more money in a month on foolishness than *daed* earns in a year."

"Oh, Caleb." Sarah's eyes filled with tears.

"I don't want your pity. I've made my choices, and I will live with the consequences." He stood. "I've answered your questions, and you have what you came for. Tomorrow I'll take you back to the bus depot. There's nothing more for you here, little sister."

He looked so angry, she felt fortunate he didn't turn her out on the street. "*Danki* for letting me stay the night."

Perhaps it was her use of a *Deutsch* word, but his expression turned sad. He looked far older than his twenty-four years. "You take my bedroom and I'll sleep on the couch. There are clean sheets in the trunk next to the bed."

When she tried to protest, he held up his hand. "No arguing, Sarah. Go to bed. You must be exhausted from your trip, and you've worn me out with your questions." He lumbered into the bathroom and shut the door.

Sarah gathered her outer garments into a bundle and found his bedroom. After praying for an hour, sleep finally came in fits and starts. Traffic noise, barking dogs, ringing phones, and the drone of an overhead TV intruded on her dreams in bizarre fashion. When she awoke the next morning, bleary-eyed and stiff from a saggy mattress, she found Caleb clean-shaven and sipping coffee at the table. A fresh quart of milk sat next to a bag of bagels.

"Good morning. Eat some breakfast, and then you can take a shower if you like. My friend Pete will pick us up at eleven and drive us downtown during his lunch hour."

Sarah poured coffee, desperate for a way to spend more time with him. "Could you please show me Lake Erie before I go home, since I've come so far?"

He smiled, slowly at first. "I guess we could swing by Edgewater Park on the way."

"And the West Side Market and the Cleveland Zoo and the Museum of Art?" She broke a bagel in half and began eating.

His eyes grew round, and then he burst out laughing. "No

time for the zoo because it's way too big, and the museum's on the other side of town. But we can have lunch at the West Side Market."

Cal Beachy was a man of his word. Sarah walked the deserted beach with her *bruder* and his friend, chasing seagulls that landed in their path. She filled her lungs with clean air and tried her best to see Canada across the water. The peace and calm from the sound of waves soothed her soul. She fell in love with the beach, even in the middle of winter. At the West Side Market, Caleb hurried her past the indoor and outdoor booths. She would have loved spending time at the international food vendors, but Cal bought three bratwurst sandwiches and herded her back to the vehicle.

All too soon they arrived downtown and pulled up in front of the bus station. Cal asked Pete to wait in the truck with the engine running while he walked Sarah inside the terminal. Before she could think of another reason to delay, Caleb kissed her on the forehead, put her on the bus bound for Akron, and walked out of her life...again.

Sarah felt the pain of loss all the way home, realizing this was what her *mamm* felt many times over.

THIRTEEN

Adam glanced at the wall clock again, unable to keep his mind on his work. He replayed his last conversation with Sarah over and over in his head until he found himself changing the words to those he should have said. He had no business being short tempered with her. She had a right to visit her brother if she wanted. He just wished Caleb lived down the road instead of in a big city filled with temptation.

Whatever Caleb had seen and done in Cleveland had made him choose to stay. He'd turned his back on his family, his faith, and the Amish lifestyle for ease and comfort. He would probably give up his right arm before relinquishing his car or truck. Moonlit buggy rides down shady lanes or hiking through a newly mown pasture at dawn couldn't compare with fancy restaurants, shopping malls, and golf courses. But Caleb Beachy wasn't his concern...Sarah Beachy was.

Would she too fall in love with a culture of few rules and no expectations? Without her *daed*, the bishop, and him watching over her shoulder, she would be free to cut her hair, paint her face, and dress in the latest styles. Because Caleb earned lots of money, she could stay with him until she found employment. Cities were filled with bed-and-breakfasts, small inns, and big hotels. With her experience, she would have her pick of jobs.

Pressure built within Adam's chest until his breath came in short gasps. He was certain he was losing Sarah to a world he didn't understand…and didn't want to. And he had no one to blame but himself. Love was the one thing that kept their Plain culture and community vibrant and strong—love between a parent and child, between siblings, and between an Amish Christian and God. God was easier to obey and His Word easier to follow in their rural society. How difficult it must be for urban Christians to stay on course without reminders of Him in each misty meadow or snow-covered hill.

Then there is the love between a man and a woman.

If he'd loved Sarah enough and had revealed his deep passion, maybe she wouldn't have been so quick to leave. Her ambivalence to wedding talk, her reluctance to get baptized, and her disinterest in planning a future with him spoke louder than an English billboard painted on a red barn. His stubborn pride had kept him from facing reality—Sarah didn't love him. If she did, he wouldn't have been so easy to leave. He'd been a fool, strung along by a woman either too afraid or too kind to hurt his feelings. Either way, Adam knew he faced a lonely Christmas. And the prospect of starting over to find a wife chilled him more than the frozen fields he gazed across. He would rather spend his life alone than fall for another woman unable to return his love.

Adam mulled over his troubles all the way home. Fortunately, his smart horse had kept track of the route while he'd been distracted. He rewarded the gelding with a fifteen-minute rubdown, three carrots, and a bucket of oats. When he entered the house's dark back hallway, he tripped over something on the rug. He sprawled forward, banging his head on the doorjamb before catching his balance. "Tarnation!" he muttered to himself. "Who left this pair of skates in the middle of the hall?" He'd assumed he was alone in this part of the house or he would have controlled his temper.

He had been mistaken.

"*Mir leid*, Uncle Adam." His favorite nephew crept out from behind the door to gather up the skates. "I forgot I'd left them there to dry."

Adam ducked his head. "It's all right, Joshua. Put them in the closet out of the way." As the child scampered off with the skates, Adam limped into the kitchen, rubbing the growing knot on his forehead.

"Oh, boy, you'll probably have a shiner," said his sister. Amanda lit the kerosene lamp with a kitchen match.

"I missed the eye. Just cracked my head." He slumped into a chair.

"'Tis a blessing then. Your head can take a few hard knocks." Despite her teasing, she wrapped a cloth around some ice cubes and gently placed it on the lump.

"*Danki*," he said, taking the ice bag from her. "Where is everybody?"

"Gone off in different directions. You're late."

"Had to finish staining a walnut dining table. Why are *you* still here?" Amanda was usually the first one out of the kitchen.

"I told *mamm* I'd reheat your supper since I thought you might need somebody to talk to."

Suspicion lifted the hairs on the back of his neck. "And what would I want to talk about?"

Amanda met his gaze without blinking. "About Sarah going to Cleveland, of course."

He ran a hand through his hair, groaning. "How in the world…"

"Rebekah stopped by this afternoon. She said you were mighty upset about Sarah's trip." She lifted a plate of meatloaf, potatoes, and yellow beans from the oven and placed it before him.

Adam rose to wash his hands, eager for a reason to get away from his sister. Amanda was bossy, opinionated, and nosy. When he returned to the table, she'd poured them each a glass of milk. She sat down, primly clutching hers with both hands.

"I appreciate your reheating my supper, but if you have something else to do…" He let his words trail off.

"Nothing more important than making sure you don't make a mountain out of a molehill."

He took a long drink before saying, "No offense, Amanda, but I don't wish to discuss Sarah."

"I know you don't, but hear me out. As a woman, I understand things that you don't."

He started wolfing down his meatloaf to get the meal over with. "What do I not understand?"

Amanda focused on the wall for several seconds before answering. "You don't have an indecisive bone in your body, Adam. You made up your mind about your work, about joining the church, and about the woman you wanted to marry with little deliberation. Nothing wrong with that, but most people need to hem and haw a bit more."

"You think Sarah can't decide whether she loves me or not? Well, sister, save your breath. I figured that one out on my own." He swallowed a forkful of mashed potatoes that stuck in his throat like wallpaper paste.

"That's not what I'm saying, but there you go, jumping to conclusions again." She spoke loud enough to draw others from the living room, but blessedly they remained alone. "Sarah might love you every bit as much as you love her, but she needs time to adjust to the idea of marriage. God willing, you two will share sixty or seventy years together. She only has *one year* to be nineteen. What's the rush?"

He set down his fork, feeling emotion build in his chest.

"She wants to visit her *bruder,* Adam. Why are you assuming she's running away? Why can't you believe that decision has *nothing* to do with you?"

"I understand what you're saying, and I like your optimism, but this isn't the first time she's pulled back from me, especially when I talk about our future." He couldn't believe he was admitting his insecurities to Amanda. He might read about them next week in the Around Town column of the local newspaper.

"Fine, but the Sarah Beachy I know isn't devious or manipulative. You surely wouldn't have lasted this long in that gal's company if she wasn't fond of you."

Despite his discomfort over their discussion, Adam laughed wholeheartedly. "*Jah*, I suppose there's some truth there."

She reached over to pat his arm. "Take comfort that Sarah might be slow to commit but she's no liar. Give her time. Don't smother her with your well-intended desire to protect. Let her find her way in this world and come to you when she's ready. In the unlikelihood she chooses a separate road from yours, let her go with best wishes." Amanda again gazed at the wall, as though seeing things not in the room. "We can't possess another person. We can only love them and hope they'll love us in return."

Adam stared down at his empty plate, willing himself not to cry. Her words had broken through his thick skull and reached his heart. "Maybe cracking my head helped after all," he said without looking up. "I've been as stubborn as a mule, and only another mule can love one of them."

"You're not the first to stumble in the romance department." She carried his plate and their glasses to the sink.

"*Danki*, sister," he said, rising to his feet.

"Pray for courage and patience tonight instead of asking for an outcome beyond your control. With faith, you might just get what you're looking for." She dried her hands and left the kitchen without meeting his eye.

Adam was grateful for the good advice, but somehow he felt no different inside. She might be right, but in his gut he knew there would be no happy ending.

He walked from the overheated kitchen onto the porch. A cold moon cast its watery light across the frozen hayfields. This same moon shone over Davenport Street in Cleveland, yet he took no comfort there. Sarah would not tie her future to his. She might come home from Cleveland and might remain Amish until her dying day, but she would never become his wife.

Thanks to Amanda's counsel, he wouldn't make a fool of himself. He'd actually considered hiring a car to drive him to Caleb's. He would have asked…no *demanded* that she come back and stop her nonsense. He would have been the laughing stock of the district. At least he'd be able to hold up his head when he crossed paths with Sarah in the future.

She was like an eagle that soared high on the wind currents, touching down only to eat and sleep. Her heart yearned for freedom—the one thing he couldn't offer.

What would an eagle possibly see in a plow-pulling mule like him?

Guilt washed over Cal like a heavy spring rain after Sarah boarded her bus and smiled at him through the tinted window. He should have invited her to stay a few days, long enough to see the zoo and visit the international stalls at the West Side Market. He should have taken her to the art museum to see paintings from artists long dead. Who knew when she would have another opportunity to sightsee? Instead, he'd hustled her back to Wayne County as though he was ashamed of his little sister. The only shame he felt was with himself.

Seeing Sarah as an adult, instead of his *bleed madchen*, had broken his heart. He'd missed watching his *schwestern* grow up. He'd missed the loving support of a family. He was cut adrift in Cleveland with little human contact other than Pete. After five years, he was no more a member of this community than if he'd settled on Mars. A person needed money—a big bank account or at least a good-paying job—to become viable in the English world. Without cash, a man was invisible in a society based on net worth. He should have saved more instead of squandering his paychecks, yet he couldn't blame *Englischers* for his foolishness.

Money was important in Amish society too. The days of bartering bushels of grain to pay the doctor were long gone. Property taxes and medical bills meant households needed to generate cash each month. But an Amish family could still live a joyous life, even if considered poor by twenty-first-century standards.

More than wanting Sarah to stay, he had yearned to board the bus with her. His taste of being English had grown bitter over the years, but home was one place he could never go. How could he look into his parents' eyes knowing the things he had done?

Don't be drunk with wine, because that will ruin your life. Instead, be filled with the Holy Spirit. Yet he'd gotten drunk too many times to count.

Don't you realize that your body is the temple of the Holy Spirit, who lives in you and was given to you by God? Yet he sported a tattoo with the name of a woman who'd broken up with him long ago.

Run from sexual sin! No other sin so clearly affects the body as this one does. Yet he'd slept with several women and was not married to any of them. He had once memorized these verses and then not lived by them.

Shame and revulsion filled him with the same nausea as the spoiled egg fu yong. God might be able to forgive those who didn't know any better—those who'd never heard the Word of God—but he *had* known better. He'd been raised to believe the wages of sin is death.

Suddenly, the blare of a horn startled Cal from his stupor. His sister's bus had departed on its way back to Canton while he stood in the middle of a slushy parking lot stewing over things better off forgotten. He couldn't change the past. His behavior doomed him to a lonely life where he didn't belong, and he shuddered to contemplate his fate when this life was over.

"Let's go, Beachy!" Pete hollered from the terminal doorway. "My truck's in the drop-off zone and my lunch hour is over. I gotta get back to work."

"Sorry. Long goodbyes—you know how it is with women."

Once back on the street, Cal wouldn't accept a ride home. Pete had done enough by driving them downtown on a workday. Cal wanted to walk to the square and ride the train home to see what Sarah had seen—the city through innocent eyes. It also would give him a chance to think. Because he couldn't return to his parents' farm, he'd better figure out a way to survive in a city without a job and without any money.

Cal exited one stop early. A positive habit he'd picked up while living in the city was running. At first he couldn't understand the appeal of jogging around the neighborhood without any place to go, but now he loved to put on sneakers and run for miles. It relieved the tension of living in an apartment with little contact with the earth. Today, ice and snow ruled out jogging, but he still could walk the city streets, finding comfort in anonymity. No one knew who he was or what he'd done. And the strangers he passed wouldn't care even if they did know.

Cal had never been in this particular area. Although not far from his apartment, this neighborhood had fared better during the real estate crash. Homes were well kept, with yards and porches decorated for the season. Christmas trees in front windows glowed with brightly colored lights. He remembered past Christmases with an ache of melancholy. Although plain and simple like the rest of their lives, an Amish Christmas was filled with good food, visits from family and friends, Bible readings of the Savior's birth, and gift giving. He hadn't received a present in five years. He would probably spend the holiday alone, slumped on his couch watching old-fashioned movies on TV.

Without warning, Cal slipped on an icy patch. Grabbing for a telephone pole with both hands, he fought to regain his balance and catch his breath. Immersed in his troubles, if not for the near fall he might have missed an unusual scene in a church front yard: Three wooly sheep grazed on a bale of hay under a rough-sawn shed. Cal blinked several times. The critters were part of the largest nativity display he'd ever seen. Joseph, Mary, three wise men, two shepherds, and an angel stood around a wooden manger. Unable to look away, Cal thought about the blessed event two thousand years ago with a pang of tender remorse.

Just as he resumed walking, one shepherd raised a hand to scratch his nose. "Good golly," Cal cried. "You're alive."

His exclamation drew smiles from the other participants. "That we are, son," said the angel.

Cal crept closer. "You don't have a real baby in there, do you?"

A grin bloomed across Mary's face. "Come see for yourself."

He walked over and peered down at a plastic doll. "Thank goodness. You had me worried." Cal straightened and stepped back. "This is a really good idea. How long will you be out here tonight?"

The angel with long white robes and flowing blond hair lifted his noble chin. "We're not supposed to speak, but I'll make an exception for you. Our shift lasts for two hours, and then other parishioners will replace us. We'll be here every night through Christmas Eve. Blessings to you, young man, on this joyous season." With a nod, his face regained its stony pose.

Cal took one last perusal and hurried on his way. But the impact of the live nativity stayed with him long into the night, as he tossed and turned while sleep refused to come.

FOURTEEN

Sunday Morning

Cal sipped his coffee and watched folks trailing into the Catholic church across the street. Although their comings and goings had never intrigued him before, today he studied the expressions of contentment, anticipation, and even joy filling their faces—emotions long absent for him. He stared for ten minutes until no more late arrivals entered the three-story stone church with soaring bell tower.

Without pausing to contemplate his actions, he pulled on his coat and ran down two flights of steps to street level. He didn't stop running until he had crossed the street and opened the pine bough-festooned front door and entered the sanctuary. He quietly slipped into the back row, far to the right, and glanced around. The interior of the church caused his jaw to drop. He couldn't imagine the existence of such grand and ornate buildings, let alone a house of the Lord. The ceiling soared into carved, curved rafters as lifelike statues of saints stood sentinel from every nook and alcove. A beatific Mary, holding the baby Jesus, smiled down on the congregation with grace, while rows of small candles burned at her feet.

Growing up in a community that worshipped God in folks'

living rooms and outbuildings, Cal was shocked by the opulence. Most striking were the enormous windows, each depicting a scene from the Savior's life, although many Cal didn't recognize from his father's Bible reading. The stained glass drew his attention with near-hypnotic power. When the congregation stood to sing, kneeled to pray, or sat to listen to the sermon, Cal caught only bits and pieces. Instead, his mind wandered back to his own Christian upbringing—praying beside his bed, listening to Scripture around the woodstove, and attending church services with people who loved him. He closed his eyes and remembered how many times his prayers had been answered and the comfort he'd received from his faith. His memories of a rural world seemed ages ago. When he opened his eyes and glanced around, most had gone except for a few still on their knees in prayer.

"I'm Father Al. May I sit with you?" Without hesitation, a man in a long black robe and high white collar sat down next to him.

Cal quickly sat up straight. "You clearing folks outta here?"

The priest smiled, deepening the web of wrinkles around his eyes. "Not at all. Please stay as long as you like. I saw you looked troubled and thought you might like to talk."

"Why would you want to talk to me? I don't go to church here."

He laughed softy. "Because it's my job to help people, whether or not they are parishioners or even Catholic."

"Tell me something, then. Why is this place so over-the-top fancy? I grew up Amish and never saw anything like this."

The priest leaned back in the pew and studied the surroundings. "I suppose this would be pretty overwhelming to an Amish man."

"I said I grew up Amish. I'm not anymore," Cal snapped. "I'm nothing now." He arched his back while his hands clenched into fists.

"That's where you're wrong, son. In the eyes of the Lord, you're certainly not nothing. Once you've known Him, and more to the point, He's gotten to know you, you'll never be forgotten."

Cal wanted to argue with this man in odd clothes, but nothing came out when he opened his mouth to speak. He stared down at his chapped and calloused hands.

"What drew you here this morning?" the priest asked. "Why did you come inside St. Stephen's?"

"Because everybody coming to your church looked happy. I haven't felt that way in a long time." Cal's words were little more than a whisper. "I wanted to know what was going on that made folks so all-fired eager to come."

"I would like to say it's the rousing sermons, but more likely it's the season. It's impossible *not* to get fired-up when we remember God sent His only Son to earth that we may be saved—that through our steadfast faith in Him, we can one day enjoy the rewards of heaven."

There it is, the same basic principle taught by the ministerial brethren, here in a place looking like a king's palace. "God wouldn't be too happy about your church spending money on fancy decorations when so many are suffering out there." Cal gestured toward the street and spat out bitter words borne of frustration.

The priest's expression revealed surprise but not outrage. "Sounds like you're angry, son. Whom are you mad at?"

"The job market, my mess of a life...mostly me, I guess." Resentment drained away as quickly as it had appeared.

The priest placed his hand on Cal's shoulder. "Then what's

keeping you here? If city life holds nothing for you, why not go home?"

Cal released a weary sigh. "I can't go home. You don't know what I've done. One night I drank an entire six-pack and passed out on the couch, sleeping all night in my clothes." In a barely audible voice he continued, "I haven't prayed or opened my Bible in ages. I haven't kept myself pure for marriage, and I'm a disgrace to my family."

Several long moments passed before the priest spoke as the magnificent church grew deathly quiet. "Do you think you're the only Christian who has ever sinned? Do you think you have done so much wrong that your parents could never forgive you? Do you think *God* can never forgive you? Because I assure you, if you are penitent, God will hear and answer prayers for forgiveness. God the Father, the Holy Spirit, and our Savior Jesus are the same here in St. Stephen's as back home. Just close your eyes, still your mind, and listen with your heart."

Cal couldn't speak. He could barely breathe. His throat had swelled with a burning tightness. Tears he'd been holding back since the priest sat down filled his eyes. He didn't want Father Al to see his weakness. *I am a grown man, not a* boppli.

For the first time in years, a *Deutsch* word had come to mind instead of English. He hadn't forgotten the dialect of his childhood. Memories of his *mamm* and *daed* flooded back, with her gentle words and his guiding hands. No longer able to contain his emotions, Caleb bowed his head and wept. The priest squeezed his shoulder once more and silently crept away. Tears flowed uncontrollably down Cal's face, washing away the last vestiges of his arrogance, pride, and shame.

"Sarah, are you up?" Elizabeth called up the steps. "A little help, please, but I just want you."

Sarah smiled patiently at Rebekah, who felt left out because *mamm* kept requesting Sarah alone. Elizabeth had had few questions about Caleb when Sarah had first returned late Tuesday evening. By the time Mrs. Pratt had picked her up at the station and driven her home, it had been almost eight o'clock. *Mamm*'s questions had required a simple yes or no.

"Was your *bruder* happy to see you?" *More shocked than overjoyed.*

"How did you like Cleveland?" *Loved the lake, the downtown skyscrapers, and the West Side Market, but Caleb's apartment wasn't fit for our sow and piglets.*

"Did Caleb look well?" *Jah, unless you counted thirty pounds thinner, eyes that looked everywhere except into another person's, and his garish snake-infested tattoo advertising someone named Kristen.*

But Sarah hadn't mentioned any of that. She'd given little information about Caleb without outright lying. And *mamm* had seemed content with her abbreviated explanation. She'd been so happy that Sarah had returned that she hugged her like a bear, kissed her twice, and sent her to bed with a mug of hot cocoa. But over the next several days, Elizabeth's curiosity about Caleb's life had gotten the best of her while ironing in the kitchen, sewing by the fire, or hanging clothes on the back porch. Slowly, Sarah had been forced to admit Caleb was unemployed, broke, not eating properly, didn't attend church, and had few friends. Yet she couldn't reveal the things he'd done that kept him from coming home. Better for their mother to believe Caleb was experiencing a rough patch than know he'd grown hopelessly dissolute during the past few years.

Sarah finished pinning her hair into a tight bun, slipped on her *kapp*, and went downstairs. *"Guder mariye."*

Elizabeth stood at the stove, frying bacon. "About time, young lady. Please start scrambling the eggs. Folks need to eat so we can leave for the preaching service. The hosting family lives an hour away."

"Do you suppose the Troyers will be there?" Sarah asked, breaking eggs into a bowl.

"Don't know why they wouldn't be. Is that what took so long—taking extra care before you see Adam?" She clucked her tongue. "I thought I smelled something peachy when you walked into the kitchen."

Sarah felt herself blush. *"Jah,* I used some scented body lotion. I need to make a good impression." She whisked milk and fresh mushrooms into the eggs.

"It's only been a week since you last saw him, not six months." Elizabeth transferred bacon strips onto paper towels to drain.

"True, but we argued at our last meeting, and I wasn't very nice to him. We didn't leave things on good terms."

"Oh? Do you wish to tell me why you argued?"

"He didn't want me to go to Cleveland. And when I said I was going anyway, he said he would come along to keep me safe." Sarah couldn't meet her mother's gaze. "I told him I didn't want him to accompany me."

Elizabeth pivoted to face her. "Oh, Sarah, that's not like you to be so insensitive."

"I know. Now I'm anxious to make amends before he replaces me with a fiancée not so mean spirited." She placed a lid on the pan and walked over to the counter to pour a cup of coffee, needing to get everything off her chest before the family came downstairs. "I told him I wanted to find out why Caleb left us."

Elizabeth looked white as a bedsheet as she turned back to the stove. After a moment she asked, "And did you find out, daughter?"

"*Jah*. It was all about the money he could make on English construction crews. He found out how much union carpenters earned and couldn't resist. He did quite well for a couple of years."

Her *mamm* snorted. "Money—love of the almighty dollar has led many young men to ruin. Perhaps someday his gold will lose its luster and he'll be back." She dried her hands on her apron with a face looking years younger than yesterday. "I'll call your *daed* in from chores so we can eat. The Beachys aren't sashaying into church late."

Sarah set the table and then poured tall glasses of milk. There was no way she could admit Caleb's gold had already tarnished and disappeared long ago. It wasn't easy money separating him from his family but specters of shame and regret. However, she had dwelled on her *bruder*'s woes long enough. Today, she must find the path of reconciliation back to Adam, if it wasn't already too late.

As much as she enjoyed worship services, especially during Advent when the ministers read the Christmas story from all four Gospels, she couldn't wait for church to be over. She hadn't seen Adam beforehand, and she couldn't locate him in the men's rows. If he hadn't come today, when would they find a chance to mend fences?

Finally, while the ladies carried hot food from the house to the barn for the noon meal, she spotted him talking with a group of men on the porch. Sarah approached until certain Adam had seen her and then waited until Samuel finished a long-winded story.

"Good afternoon, Miss Beachy," said Adam, coming down

the steps. "I see you've returned to Wayne County after all." His expression remained placid and unreadable.

"Of course I've come back. There never was any doubt."

"And what did you think of Cleveland?"

"Big, slushy, beautiful town square, lots of empty houses, and a wonderful lake with hundreds of seagulls." Nervous anxiety made her breath catch in her throat.

"And your brother—did you find him? Is he faring well?" Adam walked a step closer.

"*Jah*, I found him at his last address, but he's not doing as well as he would like. He's fallen into some bad habits, I'm afraid."

"I'm sorry to hear that." He stepped out of earshot from those on the porch, looking saddened by her news.

"But I don't want to talk about Caleb, at least not right now." Her forehead and back began to perspire despite temperatures in the thirties. "I want to talk about us, Adam. I'm sorry I've been so standoffish. I *do* wish to be your girl. That is, if you haven't already replaced me with someone less wishy-washy."

His face melted into a grin as he reached for her hand. "I thought I'd give you another year before rushing out to find a replacement. While you were seeking answers from Caleb, my sister explained a few things to me. Apparently, decisiveness and determination can easily become inflexibility and intolerance."

Sarah's eyes widened. "Who taught you this?"

"Amanda," he said with a twinkle in his cornflower blue eyes. "She's taken me under her wing in the romance department." He pulled her to his side.

"Amanda Troyer is giving courting advice?" she asked, leaning into his shoulder. "Well, this is the season for miracles, no?"

"It is. Let's get in line for lunch. My appetite has mysteriously returned with a vengeance."

"One more minute," she pleaded, not ready to join the others yet. "I decided something else on the bus ride home—I want to become baptized and join the church." Voicing the words aloud caused a flutter of nerves in her stomach. She glanced into his face with anticipation.

He lifted one eyebrow. "*Jah?* But I heard that class was filled up and there wouldn't be another for at least a year. Looks like you'll have to wait." He patted her shoulder.

"What?" she squawked. "I never heard of such a thing! Maybe I can take classes in another district. Or maybe the bishop will—"

Adam pressed a finger to her lips. "I'm teasing, Sarah. While you were in Cleveland, I found a sense of humor. There was a perfectly fine one lying on the side of the road that someone had thrown out…"

While he rambled Sarah bent down for a handful of wet snow, which she shaped into a ball. "I'll give you a three-second head start, and then I suggest you take cover, Adam Troyer." She packed the snowball tightly between her fingers.

With a laugh, he ran a zigzag pattern across the yard, but Sarah's snowball still found its mark squarely in the middle of his back.

And she'd found her mark here in Fredericksburg, Ohio. She'd grown lonesome for home during her brief time away, but absence had especially made her heart grow fonder for Adam. He was more than a good man—he loved her, and it'd taken a heartbreaking peek into Caleb's sorrowful life to realize that she loved him too. Sometimes a person didn't appreciate the goodness the Lord has bestowed until it was *almost* gone.

FIFTEEN

Christmas Eve

Sarah heard the commotion in the kitchen and knew Adam had arrived. He was taking her to the schoolhouse for the Christmas program. She'd barely had time to change her clothes after helping Mrs. Pratt all morning. Although no guests had stayed the previous night and none were expected today, Country Pleasures Bed-and-Breakfast was filled with people. Mrs. Pratt bustled around her kitchen like a bee in spring clover. Her daughter and family pulled up the driveway yesterday afternoon, bringing a ham, stuffed turkey, and all the trimmings. Her son had rented a car at the Cleveland airport and arrived last night, also a surprise. The Pratt family would be together for Christmas. And Sarah would divide her time between the Beachys and the Troyers...if she got moving right now.

Just as her mother called her name, Sarah ran down the steps and flew into the kitchen.

"Guder nachmittag, liewi," Adam greeted, his smile filling his entire face.

She blushed. Such endearments were seldom uttered in company. "Good afternoon to you."

"Eat your lunch, daughter," commanded Elizabeth. "Have

you eaten, Adam?" She pointed to a plate filled with ham-and-cheese sandwiches already made.

"I've eaten, Mrs. Beachy, *danki*." His focus darted toward the door and back.

"May I eat mine on the way? As soon as the *kinner* have eaten lunch, they'll set up for the program. We don't want to miss a thing."

"Go on then," Elizabeth said. She took a sandwich from the plate and wrapped it in a napkin. "Christmas comes but once a year." Her face shone with joy. "And don't forget to bring Katie home. No sense in her walking while you've got a buggy. And Adam, I expect you to stay for supper tonight since I'm losing my girl to your mother's good cooking tomorrow."

He nodded in agreement. Sarah kissed her *mamm*'s cheek, and then they hurried out the door. During the ride to the schoolhouse, Adam filled her ear with the young Troyer preparations for the annual event. New carols had to be learned, red-and-green paper chains hung from the ceiling, and lines had to be practiced until they could be recited without a stutter. Sarah loved Adam's devotion to his nieces and nephews.

He would make a great father.

And with God's help, she would make a good mother.

When they entered the schoolroom of eight mixed grades, Sarah's heart leaped with delight. The girls had strung cutout letters spelling "Merry Christmas" across the room and drawn Christmas scenes in colored chalk on the board. Boys had set up folding chairs and benches for parents, *dawdis* and *mammis*, and the English friends who'd been invited. She felt proud to be part of the love filling the room.

Just as she and Adam found seats, the teacher rang the bell on her desk and everyone grew quiet. A small girl stepped from behind a makeshift curtain to recite a poem about the baby Jesus. The child focused solely on Sarah during her recitation. With a start, Sarah recognized the youngest of Adam's nieces, the one who'd placed the coals for the snowman's mouth. Two skits came next—one in English by the older scholars and another in *Deutsch* by the younger students. Christmas carols then filled the room as everyone joined in the singing.

Unexpectedly, Sarah's eyes brimmed with tears as they sang "Silent Night," her favorite. As the children exchanged small gifts, she fought back waves of emotion threatening to ruin her afternoon. *Why do I want to cry watching* kinner *exchange books, colored markers, fruit, and candy?*

Perhaps because she had so easily dismissed this future for herself. Now she yearned for a family of her own more than anything, if it wasn't too late.

At the program's conclusion, several of his nephews ran to greet Uncle Adam. Joshua threw his small arms around Adam's neck and hugged.

Lydia Troyer, his eldest niece, approached their seats. "*Danki* for coming today, Sarah," she said shyly.

Sarah recalled that his niece had called her "Aunt Sarah" the day they had built the snowman. Why had she dropped the fond address? Sarah reached out to squeeze the girl's shoulders. "You're welcome. You did a good job during the skit, speaking your lines calmly and clearly."

Then Sarah spotted her little *schwester* standing by the window eating an orange. She hurried to commend Katie's performance too during the skit and singing. Katie chattered for a few moments about her many flubs during practice sessions over the last few days. Yet her solo stanza of "Joy to the World" had been flawless. Katie showed Sarah her sack of gifts, including a book on wildflowers, trail mix, and soaps shaped like hearts.

All too soon people began collecting belongings and putting on cloaks and bonnets. While Katie ran off to bid her friends "Merry Christmas," Sarah noticed Amanda standing near the door with her beau. She'd also come to see her nieces and nephews, yet she was staring at Sarah with a grin on her face.

Blushing, Sarah approached Adam's sister. "It was *wunderbaar, jah?*" she asked.

"Truly was. It filled me with the joy of the season. That, and seeing you and my *bruder* patched up."

Sarah's blush deepened to crimson. "Seeing my *bruder* made me appreciate my blessings all the more."

Amanda pulled her into a tight embrace. "With a little training and some patience, Adam should make a right fine *ehemann.*" The two women shared a hearty laugh. "I'll see you tomorrow for Christmas dinner," Amanda said as she slipped out with her fiancé.

Sarah herded Katie to Adam's buggy along with Joshua and his parents, who had walked to the school. With so many people in the small surrey, she didn't think Adam would attempt any private conversation during the ride. She was mistaken.

While Joshua described the morning's preparations from the backseat, Adam leaned close to her ear. "You seemed to have enjoyed yourself this afternoon."

"I did. *Danki* for escorting me this afternoon." She focused on the road ahead, which blessedly had little traffic tonight. "And thanks for not trying to stop me from visiting Cleveland," she added in a whisper.

"I had no right to do that even if I wanted to, which for a while I did."

Sarah shifted on the seat, feeling her palms grow clammy.

"Did you find what you were looking for in Cleveland?" he asked.

"*Jah*, and it broke my heart when I saw how Caleb was living—not the grand life we'd assumed since he'd landed a good job. Apparently, jobs come and go with the weather, and he wasn't left with much when his dried up."

"Then he should have swallowed his pride and come home. He hadn't joined the church yet. He would have been accepted back, and in time everything would have been forgotten."

Adam sounded short tempered, and Sarah regretted bringing up the subject. She dared not mention the burden of guilt Caleb carried. Adam might resent him all the more. "He had his reasons," she murmured, turning to watch the scenery.

Adam grunted for a final comment on the topic and then remained quiet for the rest of the drive.

Is he wondering what sort of evil Caleb had fallen into? Does my bruder's shame reflect on me?

When the buggy stopped in front of the Troyer house, Joshua and Katie jumped out to play in the snow. Adam's brother and wife bid her goodnight as they walked arm in arm toward the house. Sarah remained where she was, uncertain and uncomfortable, while Adam began unhitching the horse.

"Have you forgotten me? I still need a ride home. And I thought you were eating dinner with my family tonight." Her voice sounded weak and childlike.

Adam leaned his head back into the buggy. "I thought it would be more romantic if I took you home in the sleigh. Would you like that, Sarah?"

Her heart began to pound within her ribcage. "I would love a sleigh ride, but don't forget my sister will be with us."

"Oh, I think I'll get a chance to ask a couple questions I've had on my mind, as long as Katie sits in the backseat." He winked impishly. "Why don't you gather some wool blankets while I hitch up a fresh horse? I'll be back in a hurry." To his nephew he called, "Joshua, ask your *daed* to rub down my horse so we can be off. And you can help him."

Sarah watched the child run off as her spirits soared toward heaven. *Trust the Lord's timing in all things.* If only she could patiently wait and not worry so much.

Adam disappeared into the barn with his gelding but soon returned driving the sleigh with his Percheron crossbreed, bells on the leather harness jingling. Although less than twenty degrees outdoors, warmth filled every part of her as she met Adam's gaze.

He loves me. He loves me after all.

"Katie!" she hollered. "Say goodbye to Joshua and come get your things."

"A sleigh ride!" the girl exclaimed. She grabbed her lunch box and sack of presents from the buggy and scrambled up next to Adam, hoping to wedge in for warmth.

"Crawl beneath those wool blankets in the backseat, please. Adam and I wish a little time alone."

Katie made a humorous clucking sound but did as instructed. Sarah snuggled close as Adam tucked a thick lap robe around their legs. In another moment, they were flying down the driveway onto the road.

"Whoa," he called to the horse, tugging the reins. "We don't want to get home too soon, do we?"

Seldom short on words, Sarah merely shook her head. Something had closed off her throat, rendering speech impossible.

For half a mile, Adam kept the sleigh toward the side of the road, though no traffic whizzed by due to the weather. "So,

Miss Beachy, since you've decided to join the church and remain Amish, I have a question for you." He cocked his head.

Sarah clasped her hands under the blanket. "What question would that be?"

"Would you like whole berry or jelled sauce with your turkey tomorrow?"

"What?" she croaked, her face flushing hotly.

Giggles emanated from the lump of blankets behind them.

"Cranberry sauce—which do you prefer? My *mamm* was curious."

"Um…whole berry."

"Ah, that's my favorite too." He shook the reins, sending the bells jingling.

Two or three interminable seconds spun out before he spoke again. "Since we have *that* in common, I was wondering if you would marry me? Seeing that I love you more than just about anything in this world."

For a moment the night grew still, even the sleigh bells. Then Sarah burst out laughing. "*Jah*, I'll marry you, Adam Troyer. If you didn't ask me during this sleigh ride, I was planning to ask you and take my chances. I couldn't stand the suspense any longer."

Adam pulled hard on the reins, bringing the sleigh to a stop. He leaned over and kissed her then, squarely on the mouth. A good long kiss…until Katie's giggles drew them apart.

Sarah inhaled a frigid breath. "Seeing that you love me and I love you, let's get home and tell my folks before you come to your senses. My mother will be pleased…as I am beyond words," she added softy.

"Your coming home has been my best Christmas gift ever." Adam brushed a second kiss across her cheek and then focused on the road. After releasing the brake, he glanced over his shoulder before signaling to the Percheron. "Good grief, some poor fool is walking on a night like this. Let's wait a minute and offer him a lift."

Sarah pivoted on the bench and stared into darkness. Snow was falling so hard she couldn't see a thing. Then slowly the form of a tall thin man, hunched over from the cold, came into view. Nothing about him was familiar, yet in her heart Sarah knew. "Oh, Adam," she said as snow melted on her nose and cheeks. "I believe it's my *bruder*." Throwing off the blanket she jumped down, stumbled, caught her footing, and started running down the road. "Caleb?" she called into the silent white world.

And in response she heard her name, wafting on the wind like a prayer: *Sarah*.

Slipping and sliding on pavement turned icy, her brother soon reached her side. He dropped his duffle bag to the ground, and they hugged in a cumbersome embrace.

Sarah's face was wet from tears as well as melting snowflakes. "Welcome home," she said, muffled against his damp wool coat.

"Merry Christmas, *bleed madchen*." Caleb's voice sounded raw. "I didn't think I'd get home in time. I caught the afternoon bus to Canton, and then I transferred to one headed to Apple Creek, but few folks are out tonight to hitch a ride."

She stepped back to peer at him in the near darkness. His face looked cold and haggard, but it was Caleb. "Your *bashful girl* is very happy to see you." She glanced down at his bag. "Is that all your stuff?"

"Everything worth bringing home," he answered with a laugh. "I left all the rest of my worldly possessions behind for the next tenants, providing they don't mind a three-legged table or a lumpy couch."

"You might have picked July to make this trip," said Adam,

stepping from the sleigh. "But at least you're in time for Christmas Eve. Welcome home, Caleb." He extended his hand to shake.

"You must be the lucky man my sister plans to marry," said Caleb, shaking heartily.

"Adam is my intended," said Sarah. "And only time will tell how fortunate he is. In the meantime, let's get home before you freeze to death."

Elizabeth waited by the kitchen window for Sarah, Katie, and Adam to return from the school program. Rubbing a clear patch on the glass, she hoped they hadn't dawdled at the Troyers. The snow was growing heavier by the hour. Everything was ready for dinner, keeping warm in the oven. *My beef roast and baked potatoes will be dry as corn stalks if we don't eat soon.* The solar-powered light on the barn revealed nothing but swirling, driving snow. Adam would bunk at their house and go home safely in the light of day on Christmas morning.

Tonight was Christmas Eve—the night two thousand years ago that God sent His Son to earth that all who believe might be saved. She bowed her head to whisper words of gratitude for the gift of eternal life.

She'd been praying a lot lately. Sarah had returned from Cleveland after the briefest of visits—the city holding little appeal for her practical daughter. Elizabeth couldn't have borne losing another child to the English world. God had heard and answered her prayer.

How great is the Lord's mercy, especially on someone as undeserving as myself. Even the rough patch between Sarah and Adam appears to be smoothed over. What a good match they will make!

"Thank You, Lord," she whispered again. Then, with full faith and confidence, Elizabeth began removing the casserole pans from the oven. "Rebekah," she called, "pour the drinks and set cold food on the table. Your sisters and Adam will be here soon." She carried the Dutch oven to the counter. "Eli, can you spare a minute to slice the beef while I the heat the gravy?"

"How did you know, *mamm*?" Rebekah asked, entering the kitchen. "I just saw them turn up the driveway from the front window. Adam brought Sarah home in his sleigh—isn't that romantic?" She headed toward the back hall, but Elizabeth grabbed her arm.

"No, daughter, you set the table. I'll greet them myself." With a strange feeling growing in the pit of her stomach, Elizabeth shrugged on her cloak and bonnet with trembling hands. A blast of cold wind hit her face as she opened the door and walked out onto the porch. A sleek black sleigh, complete with two strings of harness bells, was parked near the barn. Adam was unhitching the horse while the two girls fought their way toward the house, bent low against the blowing snow. As Elizabeth studied the approaching figures, she realized there weren't two but three people struggling up the slippery path.

Suddenly, she felt weak in the knees as a cry escaped her lips. "Caleb," she called as he stepped into the pool of light streaming from the kitchen window.

"*Mamm*," he said. "It's...it's good to see you."

"My son." Elizabeth wrapped her arms around her firstborn and hugged tightly. Her knees didn't give way after all. She could have borne his weight along with her own and an additional fifty pounds as she was lifted up with a mother's strength and power.

"Are you here for a visit?" she asked when they released their embrace. Sarah and Katie crowded around with ear to ear smiles.

"No," he said simply. "If you'll take me back, I've come home." He waited, gazing into her eyes with naked, raw pain.

The sight of his sorrow nearly broke her heart. Elizabeth stared at the thin, pale man who'd left Fredericksburg so filled with hope and expectation, and who had come back seeking forgiveness and mercy and most of all...love.

And on this most blessed of nights, she had plenty of those gifts to spare. "Merry Christmas, my son. Welcome home."

CHRISTMAS SUGAR COOKIES

½ cup butter
1 cup sugar
1 egg
1 teaspoon vanilla
2¼ cups flour, sifted
½ teaspoon salt
½ teaspoon baking soda
¾ teaspoon baking powder

Thoroughly cream together the butter and sugar. Add the egg and vanilla and beat again well. Sift together the flour, salt, baking soda, and baking powder. Add to the butter-and-sugar mixture and chill 2 to 3 hours.

On a lightly floured surface, roll out dough ⅛ inch thick and then cut into desired shapes. Bake at 325 degrees for 8 to 10 minutes. (If your oven is too hot, even just a little, the cookies will brown too quickly around the edges.)

Cool completely and then frost as desired.

BAKED APPLES

1 cup sugar
½ cup flour
1 teaspoon cinnamon
1 cup brown sugar
1 cup water
2 teaspoon butter
4 or more cooking apples, depending on size

Combine all ingredients except for apples and boil, stirring often, until thickened.

Peel apples, core, and cut in half. Place cut side up in a 9 x 13-inch baking pan. Pour thickened sugar mixture over apples and bake at 350 degrees for 30 to 45 minutes or until apples are soft.

(From *The Homestyle Amish Kitchen Cookbook*, Georgia Varozza, general editor)

CHRISTMAS CAKE

1 pound butter
1 pound light brown sugar
6 eggs
4 cups flour, sifted
1 teaspoon baking powder
2 tablespoons nutmeg
½ cup orange juice
3 cups chopped pecans
1 pound pale yellow seedless raisins

Cream together the butter and sugar. Add the eggs, 2 at a time, and beat until very light and mixture doesn't look grainy (takes about 20 to 25 minutes total). Sift together the flour, baking powder, and nutmeg. Add gradually to the creamed mixture and beat until well blended. Stir in orange juice or blend in using lowest speed on mixer. Fold in the pecans and raisins.

Pour the cake batter into a 10-inch tube pan that has been greased and floured. Bake at 300 degrees for 1 hour and 45 minutes.

Remove the cake from the oven and cool for 10 minutes. Then turn the pan over and let the cake slip out gently. Cool completely. Wrap tightly and store for at least a week because it tends to be crumbly when fresh.

(From *The Homestyle Amish Kitchen Cookbook*, Georgia Varozza, general editor)

ABOUT THE AUTHOR

Mary Ellis grew up close to the eastern Ohio Amish Community, Geauga County, where her parents often took her to farmers' markets and woodworking fairs. She and her husband now live in Medina County, close to the largest population of Amish families, and enjoy the simple way of life.

Sarah's Christmas Miracle is Mary's first Christmas novella. She is also the author of the bestselling Miller Family series, which consists of *A Widow's Hope, Never Far from Home,* and *The Way to a Man's Heart.*

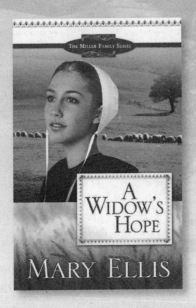

A WIDOW'S HOPE

Can a Young Amish Widow Find Love?

After the death of her husband, Hannah Brown is determined to make a new life with her sister's family. But when she sells her farm in Lancaster County, Pennsylvania, and moves her sheep to Ohio, the wool unexpectedly begins to fly. Simon, her deacon brother-in-law, finds just about everything about Hannah vexing. So no one is more surprised than the deacon when his own brother, Seth, shows interest in the beautiful young widow.

But perhaps he has nothing to worry about. The two seem to be at cross-purposes as often as not. Hannah is willful, and Seth has an independent streak a mile wide. But much is at stake, including the heart of Seth's silent young daughter, Phoebe. Can Seth and Hannah move past their own pain to find a lasting love?

An inspirational story of trust in the God who sees our needs before we do.

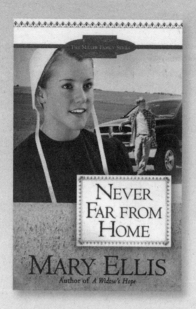

NEVER FAR FROM HOME

What Happens When an Amish Girl's
Prince Charming Is an Englischer?

Emma Miller is on the cusp of leaving childhood behind and enter-ing the adult world. She has finished school, started her own wool business, and longs for someone to court. When the object of her affec-tion is a handsome English sheep farmer with a fast truck and modern methods, her deacon father, Simon, knows he has more than the farm alliance to worry about.

Emma isn't the only one with longings in Holmes County. Her mother yearns for relief from a debilitating disease, Aunt Hannah wishes for a baby, and Uncle Seth hopes he'll reap financial rewards when he under-takes a risk with his harvest. But are these the plans God has for this close-knit Amish family?

An engaging story about waiting on God for His perfect timing and discovering that dreams planted close to home can grow a lasting har-vest of hope and love.

THE WAY TO A MAN'S HEART

Can a Loving Amish Woman
Be a Refuge for a Wounded Soul?

Leah Miller, a talented young woman in the kitchen, is living her dream come true as she invests in a newly restored diner that caters mostly to locals. Jonah Byler is a dairy farmer with a secret. Having just moved to the area, can he persuade this quiet young woman to leave her adoring fans and cook only for him? Once she discovers what he has been hiding from others, can Leah trust Jonah with her heart?

Working at the diner introduces Leah to both Amish and English patrons. Though maturing into womanhood, *Rumschpringe* holds little appeal to the gentle, shy girl who has never been the center of attention before. When three Amish men vie for her attention, competing with Jonah, Leah must find a way to understand the confusing new emotions swirling around her.

A captivating story that lovingly looks at how faith in God and connection with family can fill every open, waiting heart to overflowing.